# G
# INTO THE ABYSS

---

"An intriguing, haunting fever dream at the world's end."
**KIRKUS REVIEWS**

"Dalan Musson has imagined a most unusual modern western
set on the edge of the end of civilization. In lean, pointed
prose, he transports us to a brutal world where everything is
in tatters—including our own idea of heroism. Blood will be
spilled. Ideals will be destroyed. Yet, what makes his writing
exceptional is that in decay and despair, in moments where the
brave (or the merely bold and stupid) decide to press on against
the odds, Musson unearths the last thing we'd ever expect to
find: kindness, empathy, and even a dash of hope."
**AMY NICHOLSON**
**FILM CRITIC**
**AND CO-HOST OF THE UNSPOOLED PODCAST**

"A crackling debut. Musson's haunting exploration of faith
echoes the best of Cormac McCarthy. I can't stop thinking
about it."
**KIRK WALLACE JOHNSON**
**AUTHOR OF THE FEATHER THIEF**

---

# GAZE LONG
## INTO THE ABYSS

# GAZE LONG
## INTO THE ABYSS

Dalan Musson

A California Coldblood Book
Los Angeles, Calif.

THIS IS A GENUINE CALIFORNIA COLDBLOOD BOOK
Los Angeles, Calif.

californiacoldblood.com

Set in Minion
Cover design by Dale Halvorsen

Printed in the United States

Publisher's Cataloging-in-Publication Data

Names: Musson, Dalan, author.
Title: Gaze long into the abyss / Dalan Musson.
Description: Los Angeles, CA: California Coldblood Books, 2023.
Identifiers: ISBN: 978-1-955085-14-4 (paperback) | 978-1-955085-15-1 (ebook)
Subjects: LCSH Dystopias--Fiction. | Survival--Fiction. | Rapture (Christian eschatology)--Fiction. | Disasters--Fiction. | West (U.S.)--Fiction. | Horror fiction. | Apocalyptic fiction. | BISAC FICTION / Science Fiction / Apocalyptic & Post-Apocalyptic. | FICTION / Horror
Classification: LCC PS3613.U844 G39 2023 | DDC 813.6--dc23

## DEDICATION

*For Allison. Twice.*

## 1. The Old Man

**IT MIGHT HAVE BEEN MORNING,** but it was hard to tell.

It was always dark, these days ... and "these days" had been every day for a long, long time. A hoary pallor when it was supposed to be light, an eerie, ominous glow high up somewhere when it was supposed to be dark. None of it would have been so bad if it ever changed. If there was ever a difference. If there was ever anything else.

A thunderstorm raged in the distance. That, too, was always the same. It never moved. It hung, it threatened, but it never moved. Stayed close enough to cause a twinge of concern in the back of one's head, just enough to make a man worry about what might come. Just enough to wake you up with a roll of noise in the middle of the night, make you sit up and ask yourself if it was finally here. Enough that you couldn't quite get your eyes to close again, sitting there thinking about it, listening, just in case the rain started.

But it was there. Off in the distance. Always there.

Here, though ... What about here? Here was what passed for a homestead. Built of well-worn timbers, barely held together by rusted nails and mumbled prayers. It was small. Made smaller by a trick of what light there was, its shadow barely cast on the dusty ground outside.

It sat in the middle of a field, the way any point can be the "middle" of something if you're so inclined. But the field wasn't much more than the homestead, which wasn't much more than the sky, which is to say, none of it was much of anything. Not much of anything good, at least. Not by the way things ought to be judged.

All around the homestead, stretching out for whatever distance a man used these days, were haphazard traces of what used to be crops. Most of them were barely more than marks in the fallow, a reminder that something may have once grown there. Now, if the thunderstorm had got closer, dared to threaten rain, maybe that threat could be seen as a promise, as a hope. It might have given the land a chance. Something to wait for. But the rain never came. And the land here, as it was everywhere as far as anyone knew, was parched, dry and barren.

The pigs knew it, too. Seven of them in a lazy pen that was barely a suggestion of where they were supposed to stay. But where would they go anyway? Even a man who'd never seen pigs before, never heard of the animal, hadn't the slightest clue what a pig was supposed to look like, could tell  this wasn't it. Every day was a miracle, that the pigs may stretch out their meager existence a bit longer, that whatever malady had hold of them and damn sure wasn't ever going to let go, stayed its grip for another hour. Still, they clung to life the way animals do, without consideration or worry. They simply were.

The sky, the ground, the house, the pigs. Whatever the material, there was no material difference. Everything was dying. And inside the homestead was worse, if such a thing were possible.

THE OLD MAN SITS UP on the small, rickety bed. His legs hang over the side, barely scraping the floor. He's not a tall man, and it's not a tall bed.

Sitting up is a war against his body, with his shoulders stooped and his head bowed, the weight of the world pushing down on him from above and slightly behind, forcing him down, ever farther.

His scraggly beard hasn't been maintained in so long it's stopped bothering to grow, and the rest of his patchy hair is all different lengths, like it was cut by a child who quit halfway through. There's a lifetime of work in his rough hands, noticeable as they move up to rub the rheum out of his tired eyes. The hands are calloused and worn, still strong, the only part of that body what still worked right. And as he rubs those eyes, forces himself to open them and face another damn day, we see the scars.

Jagged and rough, scattershot, the scars cover his forehead and temples. They're old wounds by now, and even in their advanced age it's clear they ain't come from a fight—there's too many of them, for a start. This was some terrible accident, like falling into brambles and being forced to claw your way out. This was painful, deep hurt from long ago, and the time since hadn't been kind. The scars were a part of him, but they moved and bent with a life their own as the Old Man finally stood up. He moved slowly, like a man ashamed. Each step the agony of the years catching up to him, each step the ground fighting back against being trod on. Each breath the air winning its long war against life.

Above the bed, something easy to miss: a cross. Handmade. Two small pieces of wood, notched, fit, and lashed together. If you looked close, and knew what to look for, you'd see the rope was frayed and stretched, dried with age. And whether you knew what to look for or not, you'd know it had been there a long, long time. But placed with care, and placed for a reason. Then you'd notice more of them, around the small home. More of them than should be necessary, even for decoration. Etched into the doors of the two small cabinets next to the bed. Nailed to a special place on a wall. Hanging from the edge of what passes for a doorway. Once you see the crosses you can't unsee them; they are everywhere. Assailing you from all sides, placed in fact so you can't avoid looking at them—even in the floor, when you look down.

But the Old Man doesn't look, down or otherwise. He is practiced at avoiding their judgment. He shuffles across the small room—barely four steps—and washes his face in a bucket filled with stale water. How long has it been sitting there, like that? It doesn't matter. And when he's finished, he doesn't look up, not that that would matter either; the mirror above the basin is covered with torn strips of paper, glued down. A tattered and torn, moth-eaten and burnt edge of fabric adds a second layer of protection against whatever might be under there.

As with the crosses, once you notice the mirror, it never leaves you. You can't help but see that both small windows are boarded over, too. Now, maybe the glass broke out some years ago and he just never got around to replacing it … but when you see the few picture frames, facedown on the mantle above the unused fireplace, you'd be right to surmise this is all connected. All done for a reason some time ago, and maybe that reason's been forgotten by now, but everything stays like this, maybe by habit, but maybe not.

Like every day, the Old Man eats standing up with the same spoon from the same bowl. Whatever that unrecognizable cold mash is, it can't taste good. And it certainly doesn't serve a purpose in the way food is supposed to, if the way the man's clothes hang off his old, beaten frame is any indication, which it almost always is. He finishes what food there is, the same way he does every morning, since it's there. He washes the bowl in that same bucket, even though the same gruel is going in the same bowl tomorrow, and it wouldn't matter much if there were dried and caked bits left in there from today. He still hasn't looked at anything—his eyes still avoid every cross on every surface—as he heads for what passes as the door.

Outside it ain't much different. He carries another portion of mash out with him and dumps it in the trough, which is still mostly full from yesterday. Pointless, really, since the pigs ain't gonna eat today, the same way they didn't eat yesterday, and likely ain't gonna eat tomorrow. Wretched things can hardly move. Maybe a nose twitches if you were to look close, but even a man who's never seen pigs before, never heard of the animal, knows this ain't how pigs ought to behave when there's a meal to be had. Whatever's left for 'em, it won't be long coming.

Before the Old Man goes, though, he takes that second look you take when you can't kick the feeling there's something you're supposed to see. One of 'em, one of the pigs … maybe, just maybe. So the Old Man kneels, takes the snout with a gentleness in those rough old hands, and he looks into those eyes. The eyes of any animal—you look into 'em, and you can see it. Whatever that something is, call it a soul, that spark of life and intelligence. You look into that poor wretch's eyes, you commune with that soul, and you know.

*Soon enough,* he says. That voice is quiet, it's tired, and it's not so much gruff because there's no malice behind it, there's just … nothing. It ain't the voice of a man the way you'd recognize it. More just a collection of sounds; no feeling, no soul. Whatever makes a voice memorable, or recognizable, is gone.

After he lets the snout down gentle, the Old Man stands, which is a lot easier than getting down was. He studies that pig another second, before that fleeting connection of two souls goes somewhere else and the pig looks away, because that moment was over. The Old Man looks away too—looks up at that thunderstorm, always off in the distance. Goddamn thing.

*Come for us all, soon enough.*

Later in the day, out in the fields, a bent and broken old plow bounces along the hard earth. It has no noticeable effect, but the Old Man keeps on, today as every day, because by now it is just the thing that is done. The day has no effect on him, the plow has no effect on the earth, and such is the way of things, today as every day.

Later still, and you could probably guess it's night because that one candle burns faintly nearby the bed; though as you might imagine the candle doesn't give off much light, much the same as nothing around here does much of anything the way it's supposed to. The Old Man doesn't need the light, as there's nothing he's doing that requires it; the candle is lit because that's just the way things are done, today as every day. And tonight, as every night, the Old Man kneels at the side of the bed, head bent, deep in whatever passes for a prayer. There's no sound, not the slightest movement, except maybe a twitching of those scars from so long ago, and you can't help but wonder if there's a memory deep in there that might be worrying its way up and out.

Later still, which you know because the candle is burnt down to nothing now, there's a crack, like you'd expect if that goddamn storm ever got here and hit with the lightning and the thunder. Except this crack is from the Old Man sitting up awake in bed, this crack is from those eyes opening in abject terror, this crack is from the drop of cold sweat rolling off one of those scars onto the timeworn sheets, and those poor things are hardly suited to soak up that little bit of moisture anymore.

The Old Man looks around, scans that room though he can't see a damn thing, wondering where the crack came from. But he knows. He knows nothing has changed, the same way nothing has ever changed, and that bastard of a sound that doesn't sound like anything else in this world didn't come from anywhere but inside him. So he goes back down and closes those eyes, but that sound ain't ever gonna let you sleep right again after that, like that last little bit of pain that never lets up, and never lets you forget about it.

**THE NEXT DAY WAS MUCH of the same.** Such was the day after that, as most of the days before that were, too. But one day— maybe it was the next day, or maybe one of the innumerable days after—it happened.

He was kneeling at the trough. One of the legs had given way, buckled under the weight … not that it mattered, because the mash stayed in the trough regardless, and the pigs didn't eat it anyway, but that's just not the way things are done. The Old Man kneeled at the trough, setting the wood in such a way that it would stand up level again on the uneven ground—

There it was, off in the distance… . No, not in the direction of the thunderstorm. At first, the Old Man didn't trust what he was thinking; nothing ever changed, and what were the chances this were gonna happen now, of all times? And while he couldn't see at this distance—no one could'a seen at this distance—but he knew what was happening; it was unmistakable: someone was coming.

They were a long way off, and wouldn't be here for a while yet, but someone was coming. So the Old Man stood, and he brought his bucket, because what else was he gonna do with it now, and he walked out past the old fence. When he found a spot as good as any, he stood and waited. The same as he washed his face in the morning, the same as he fed the pigs, or lit that damn candle before he knelt at the bed, he stood and waited. Not because he expected any particular thing to come of it, but just because that's the way things were done.

He stood. And he waited awhile. And he didn't feel any old way, no anxiety, no boredom, because he knew what was coming.

## 2. *The Kid*

HE WAS GROWN ENOUGH TO be out on his own, but young enough not to know better. And if we're being fair, he was less of a kid and more of a young man, really. But he was younger than the Old Man, and so, for now, he was a kid.

So the Kid carried on down the road, hurrying, now that he could see the homestead getting closer. He had that energy, the energy that only came from youth, when you were young and you saw something you wanted and you went straight after it, without any other kind of concern in the world. He had a fire in his eyes, like a preacher. One of those true believers that would never be swayed, no matter what was said to him, because come what may he knew what he knew, and what he knew was the Truth.

He wore something that might once have been a uniform, but it'd been worn a long time, and patched up as many times as necessary; a lot of what might have identified what it meant, and what separated the man who wore it from other men, was long gone. But it still got some life in it yet, so the Kid kept wearing it. These weren't the kind of times when you could let things go to waste. Not things that still had some life in them yet. Across'd his back was slung a rifle, old and heavy, made proper of brass and wood, fit together by hand. Not perfect, but nothing was, and in perfection's place was the fact it was made with care and caution and a mind to the work, which is the way things ought to be made. It had lasted at least a lifetime and would last a couple more without too much trouble. It was an artifact of a time long gone, a time would most definitely never be forgotten, not when young men who never knew the horrors of where those artifacts came from still carried them, with a fiery vision of what they might do with one now that it was in their hands.

There were all those thoughts, all the dreams and desires that come'a youth, running through his head, which made the distance he had to travel all that much shorter, until he realized he was there. And there, too, was the Old Man. Waiting.

The Kid stopped and stood a fair distance away—a little farther than felt natural to him, but he'd always been taught to be respectful of others and what might be their peccadillos, and that was his aim now. The Kid stood up straight, and absently smoothed out that uniform he'd been wearing for so long, as to make it and himself a little more presentable; as presentable as things ever were these days … and, well, he had no idea what the Old Man found presentable or not, but he convinced himself to stop thinking about it after a fashion.

The Kid studied the Old Man. Not that he knew what he was looking for, exactly, but he figured maybe if he just did it anyway, he'd figure out why. The Old Man studied him back. From far enough away, it looked the same, the way the two men were staring at each other. But even the Kid knew the way the Old Man looked at him was different from the way he looked at the Old Man. There was something hopeful in the Kid; the Old Man was closer to what might be seen as resignation. Because the Old Man knew what he was looking for, looking at, and knew what he would see long before he'd looked. Fact of the matter was, the Old Man didn't need to look. He just knew.

The Kid knew too. He knew there was something he didn't know, and whatever it was sat in the back of his mind, just out of reach. Even if it was something that could have been looked at, it would have been a hairsbreadth past his sight. Maddening, to know there was something, but not have the words to identify it, which meant you could never get hold of the thought and contain it. And so to combat the agony of not knowing—of not even knowing what it was exactly he didn't know—the Kid was about to say something, when …

*Bout time you showed up.* The Old Man was looking off, and the words basically appeared in the air, rather than having been spoken aloud. He didn't want to say it. Didn't want to admit to needing to say it. But there it was. It was done. They were connected, now. The words had been spoke.

… But that couldn't be right, could it? The Kid hadn't told a soul what he was doing, where he was going, or what he'd planned to do once he got wherever that was. There was no way word could have reached the Old Man—or anybody—and even a kid who hadn't seen much at all could tell no one had been here for a long, long time. And damn it all, the way he spoke those words.

*You were expecting me?* The Kid was embarrassed that it came out like a question. He was thinking it, certainly, but it was a fleeting thought that once uttered he felt he shouldn't have shared.

*Expecting someone, eventually.* The Old Man's response didn't feel right; it didn't feel like he was talking to the Kid, but instead talking to someone else, like he was filling in the details of the conversation after the fact. It was unnerving—it would have been unnerving even if the Kid wasn't a kid—and now the Kid had no idea what to say. How was he supposed to respond to a question that wasn't a question, being asked of someone that wasn't him?

*What'cha doin' here, Kid?* Like the Old Man already knew the answer, didn't want to hear it, but had to ask anyway.

The Kid fought to pull his response out from where it was tangled under him. *She said I could come this way, if I ever needed you.*

*Who's that exactly?* Goddammit, the Old Man already knew the answer. Why was he even asking? What's worse, it was like the Kid couldn't help but say. Like each question just pulled the next words straight from him.

*Mary. She was my mother,* the Kid said. And like when he'd heard that crack from the night before, or whatever night that was, the Old Man changed. Like those words were a heavy stone, hung round his neck, and whatever was pushing down on him from above and just behind now got heavier, started pressing a little bit harder.

*… Mary.* It was hard for the Old Man to even say the name aloud. *Never did I think I'd hear that name again.* He was lost for a moment, off somewhere else, off somewhen else. A cinch caught in his face—he couldn't help it—and that tightened one of the scars, and that sent him somewhence, lost again, and everything in that moment had changed. Especially when the Old Man realized, *Was?*

The Old Man looked back to the thunderstorm, that damned thing. He already knew what it meant, but he had to say the words, to make sure. And so maybe he didn't see the Kid nod, and maybe he did, but he didn't need to. It was a goddamn shame, that. Even though he'd known it was likely for a long, long time, and that weight had always hung down on him, but it was worse now.

*She said I could come this way, if I ever needed you.* The Kid repeated the words, even though he didn't need to.

And the Old Man thought maybe it was a rustle in the background, or a trick of the wind, but maybe the Kid had said *would* instead of *could*. He'd never know for sure, as was the way of things, and it didn't really matter. But what the Old Man needed to know was, *Why would you need me?*

The Kid replied without thinking. *She said you'd understand.*

*Well, I don't.* The Old Man's response meant the Kid would be forced to say it, meant the Kid would need a moment, to think, and pray, and collect himself, before he could speak the words aloud. Goddammit, the Old Man knew the answer, and the Kid knew he knew, but he was gonna make the Kid say it.

Instead, all the Kid could make with was, *What's wrong with your pigs?* But it weren't his fault, exactly—the Kid had just noticed, and it was an honest enough question, but it wasn't fooling anybody that it was supposed to buy him just one extra little second before he was gonna have to say the words.

*Same thing wrong with everything else,* the Old Man lobbed back, more to himself, to the world, than the Kid. But it still answered the question, in a way that was designed to make sure there were no other questions.

Except the Kid wasn't quite ready. Was still building up to the thing, and he tried to weasel around it with *She said you'd help me. She said you wouldn't be happy about it, but you'd help me.* And all those words were true, and the Kid was right, and the Old Man didn't take any great or small pleasure in watching the Kid squirm, but by god … if this was gonna be done, it had to be done the right way, and the Kid was gonna have to say it.

*Get on with it, Kid.* The Old Man meant it. And with that, the Kid knew he'd run as far as he could. He had to turn and face the thing, even if it was only words. But they were the worst words.

The words no one wanted to hear spoke.

*He's returned,* the Kid finally said, in barely more than a whisper. And there was only one He that could mean.

That pause … that next pause, where those words hung, it was time and space, form and void. It was everything. Even the thunderstorm way out there, even that damnable thing paused for a second and let the air go quiet.

*Can't be.* The Old Man kicked the words out, as close to angry as you might ever see him get.

*It's true.* The Kid was begging him to understand. To make him see that it was the Truth. He didn't want to have to talk about this no more. He wanted this part to be over.

*You better hope not,* the Old Man snapped, though wasn't angry with the Kid, he was angry with the Truth. But as everyone who knows a thing can tell you, there's no fighting the Truth. Once you hear it, you know, and it stays with you forever. And some of those Truths, well … they hang on you like a weight, pushing down, from just above and a little behind.

And still the Kid pleaded. He needed the Old Man to see this was one of those Truths. *Haven't you seen what's going on out there?*

*Ain't been out there in a long, long time,* the Old Man responded. And the way he said it, the Kid might'a thought the Old Man was fighting the Truth, but he wasn't. The Old Man knew the Truth, knew it before he heard it, knew it when he knew the Kid was on his way, knew it when the Kid got here, and knew it now.

*It's happening, just like they said it would,* the Kid continued, as though the Old Man needed convincing. *Just like they wrote in the Old Books.*

*Never read 'em,* the Old Man replied, and now it was as though the Kid knew he had already accepted the Truth. And so it was like the Kid and the Old Man were having two separate conversations; one about the Truth, and one about damn near anything but.

And then the Kid said something else. *He's already opened the first four Seals.*

And those words, whether they was part of that first Truth or not, those were the Truth too. And this Truth … Well, it'd been a long time since there was a Truth the Old Man didn't know, that he hadn't even considered. And both men had nothing to do but stand there for what could have been forever, while the Old Man considered everything that meant, and everything it would mean.

And after what seemed like an eternity to everyone but the Old Man, his shoulders slumped just a little more. And he sighed, resigned to the fact that *Well then, there ain't nothin' much left to do but wait for it then, is there?* And though that wasn't a question that needed answering, the second half most certainly was. *So why do you need me?*

And the Kid's answer was something the Old Man thought he might'a knew, but most certainly didn't know he knew it, until it was said. *Because I'm gonna stop Him from opening the others.* And if that weren't enough, the Kid added, *I'm gonna kill Him.*

THE OLD MAN MOVED LIKE a shot, closed that distance—the distance the Kid thought was awkward, but he was just being polite—in an instant. Faster than the Old Man should have been able to move; faster than any man should have been able to move, he had the Kid's face, there, in those rough hands. The Kid didn't have to think to pull away—instinct took over and told him to do that—but it didn't matter so much since he was held in such a way he knew he couldn't move, and so the same instinct that told him to move just told him instead to stay put. So there, like that, the Old Man studied him, like he studied them pigs, looking into the Kid's eyes like he looked into theirs, and if the Kid maybe thought it was a test of his manhood, a challenge, he would'a made damn sure not to look away, so the Old Man knew he wasn't afeared.

*You can't,* said the Old Man. There was finality in those words, and he let the Kid go at the same time the Kid decided again that he wanted to pull away.

*She said you almost did, once.* The Kid spit the words, trying to prove a point, but also trying to get some balance back on the scales of their interaction, though he was the only one keeping score.

*Yeah, well, you see where almost gets you.* And it was true. "Almost" got the Old Man here—to the homestead, what passed for a house, and the pigs, and the broken-down trough, and the land that wouldn't plow, and the corn that fit-and-started but never grew the way things were supposed to. Everything was almost, here.

But the Kid wouldn't be deterred, not now. He knew what he knew, what he aimed to do, whether it was the Truth or not—such trivialities didn't matter to him, not in moments and not in matters like this. *She said you could show me how,* he said, and the Kid's words weren't a request, and it weren't exactly a command, but it was somewhere between the two, leaning closer to the latter. And it made those scales tip just a little, whatever the Old Man heard in those words.

*I'm not sayin' he can't be stopped, kid. Sayin' you ain't the one to do it. You got no idea what it takes to stand against one such as Him*. And even the Old Man couldn't face the whole Truth held in those words, and he turned away and looked back to the storm, where the Truth and those memories and the knowing of what the Kid aimed to do all kinda roiled in the darkness together. *Leads you to a place you don't wanna be. Teaches you things you don't wanna know about yourself.* And this last part … this last part was said cold, and heavy, like it come from the clouds themselves with a roll of thunder. *And once all that's in you, it don't come out.*

The Old Man shuddered. And even the Kid, who ain't never met a man like this, and didn't know from his mannerisms and all the wherefores and whatnots of the person, knew that shudder wasn't a thing that happened lightly. But still, those scales had been tipped, just a little. And the Kid knew what he wanted, and he was still full of that fire of youth and his desires got the best of him and he lost all sense of damnable compassion when he said *Just sounds like you're scared.*

When the Old Man heard that, he turned and looked at the Kid, and there was something different in his eyes. There was that understanding, and that compassion, and that lack of fire, and all the other things that come with age and experience and knowing. And the Old Man knew what he wasn't afraid of, but he damn sure knew what he was, and one of the things he wasn't afraid of was admitting what he was. *Damn right. I seen the other side. Never want to go back.*

And then, not to tip those scales, but in the interest of finding out an answer to a question he didn't already know the answer to, the Old Man asked, *You ever fire that rifle, kid?*

And the Kid couldn't help but smile as he whipped it round like he'd practiced a million times, and slipped it free and held it out to the Old Man, just in case he was interested in seeing such a fine thing as the Kid thought it was. *Crack shot*, he let the Old Man know, not bothering to hold down the pride.

But the Old Man didn't want the rifle, he just wanted the answer. And though the Kid was proud of his answer, the Old Man surely wasn't. *Not talkin' 'bout findin' dinner, or takin' a bird when you feel like showing off. You ever fire it'n anger? Or fear? You ever look down those sights and see a man begging you not to, and do so anyway?* The Old Man's question rang hard in the Kid's ears, and there was a lifetime more Truth when the Kid didn't say anything than there ever could have been if he did.

His work done, the Truth found out, the Old Man turned, took that bucket, and headed back for the house. He called out as he walked, and the words rung just as clear as if he was holding the Kid's face and staring him in the eyes. *Stay here the night. We'll get some food in ye. Come morning, we'll get you on your way back home.*

And the Kid followed, because that's what he'd come all this way to do after all, but he felt the need to call out ahead to make sure the Old Man knew. *I'm not afraid.*

The Old Man kept walking. His response was harder to hear now, farther away, but the Kid could still feel the words cut through him when he said, *Then you definitely ain't ready.*

## 3. Inside, Later

**THE KID WAS BY HIMSELF, now.** How long he'd been like that was hard to say; long enough that he was just now starting to look around the small house. There wasn't a lot to see but still a lot to take notice of, and for one as curious as the Kid, there was a whole world in every corner of this little place. The crosses, the scuffs, all the knots in the wood, everything had a story he would love to have heard, or a hidden meaning he could lose himself in for hours trying to decipher.

His eyes kept coming back to the mirrors, covered up like they were. There had to be a reason. And maybe the reason was clear, would be clear, when he moved that thin piece of fabric out of the way. The second he touched it, that cling of dirt and grease and everything that had collected there over the years stuck to his hand, and made the Kid rethink why he'd ever done such a thing, which then itself struck him as funny if not absurd, that after everything he'd been through on the road, all the grease and grime and dirt and all the wetness and damp he'd slept in and climbed out of and all he'd been exposed to, that now, it was a piece of dirty fabric in a warm enough house with a proper floor that made him recoil and almost retreat. But he did pull back that fabric, and then had to work what was left of his nail under the edge of a piece of that paper, to try and catch a nib, big enough that he could get a decent pinch of it to pull away.

For all that work and minute focus, once the paper was caught it tore up and away easy enough. That part was surprising, since it felt like everything these days was more work than it should be. Success in this smallest of tasks left the Kid staring at his own reflection, which was surprising, too, in its own way. He'd been living so long where nothing was as he'd expected, that the fact that what was covered up was, in fact, just a mirror, well … he wasn't sure what he'd expected, but if you'd'a asked him to guess, he might'a said anything but that.

The Kid looked at that reflection awhile now. His face was dirty, and the lines in it were deeper than he'd remembered; he remembered it had been some time since he'd seen his reflection, so that in itself shouldn't have been a surprise. But the Kid, like all of us, had that internal reflection that don't always make sense with the outside one, and though he didn't feel like his face should have looked exactly like the one staring back at him, well … that was one of those Truths, he supposed.

He put the coverings back best he could, remembering his manners, and suddenly not wanting to feel like a destructive force visiting upon another. He cursed himself just under his breath—what was wrong with him, letting curiosity get the best of him like that, stead'a respecting the sanctity of how the man wanted his own house to be? What gave him the right?

Well, done was done, and with the fabric back in place the whole thing weren't much the worse for wear, and it's not like you could see much through it uncovered anyway so hopefully it would be fine now, like it hadn't been messed with in the first place. The Kid moved along, admonishing himself to only look, and not be off changing things around where it wasn't his place. So when he reached one of those picture frames, he went through it in his head, and he reasoned that it wasn't hurting anything to lift it up and look, so long as he put it back down the way he found it.

It was the Old Man, he was sure of it. A sight younger, but most definitely him. The Kid wasn't sure how he could tell, but he knew it had to be. Strange, how different the Old Man looked, without—it was the scars he was without, that's what was so different. And there, next to him: a woman. Now, the Kid wasn't all that good at bringing faces to mind, but this one looked so familiar that there was almost no way he could be mistaken. He looked closer, just to be sure, but it almost had to be …

*Ain't the best glass. Might break, you drop it like that.* The Old Man's words appeared out of nowhere and cut the mighty silence, and damn it all if the Kid didn't jerk his hand away and snap around just as he let the picture frame hit the mantle with a sound that made him pray for a second he hadn't, in fact, broken the glass.

When the Kid collected himself enough, and had buried the embarrassment of getting caught enough so he could take in what he was seeing, he wondered how the Old Man had made his way into this one small room without making a sound, and where that tattered old blanket he had been carrying, and was now laying out on the floor, had come from.

*Sorry, I didn't mean to.... I was just having a look around.*

The Old Man waved off the concern with half a glance, letting the Kid know he meant it when he said, *No harm. Can't blame the curiosity.* And now satisfied with what he'd done with the blanket, the Old Man prepared a few other things around that little area. And to be honest, even a moment later had you asked the Kid exactly what things the Old Man had done, he couldn't have told you. It didn't seem like the Old Man was one to just busy himself out of restlessness, mind you—it was clear every action had a purpose, it was just the Kid couldn't have told you what he'd done or what that purpose had been.

Unsure what to do, unsure what actions he was supposed to take, the Kid thought back to his manners, and what he was taught, and thought to ask, *So why do you live so far out here?*

He was surprised when the Old Man actually stopped a breath there, and thought about the question, like he didn't already know the answer. *Well, I suppose ...* and if the Kid weren't mistaken, the Old Man actually had to think about it, and the Kid thought that meant he'd done a good job, as far as asking questions went. *Where else would I go?*

The Kid still wasn't sure what he was to do, while the Old Man prepared his things, so he kept on talking. *I dunno exactly. Anywhere? There's a village not ten miles back. People there seem to be growing food just fine. It's not much, not compared to the way I hear things used to be, but it's … better. Better than this, that's for sure.*

The Old Man looked up, and the Kid knew maybe he'd forgotten his manners and had said too much, even though he was really just trying to be helpful. *Here's fine,* the Old Man said. *I got the pigs. And don't have much desire to see the mess people made of the world they was given.*

*We didn't do this,* the Kid snapped back. He'd remembered his manners, so he wasn't 'bout to raise his voice, but this was something he felt passionately about, and it wasn't like him to let go a slight like that. *It was Him brought all the suffering and whatnot upon us.* He held eyes with the Old Man as long as he could—which wasn't long. The Kid could tell from that look in the Old Man's eyes, he thought the Kid still had more than a little left to learn, and that's a hard look to bear for anyone, let alone a kid who thinks he knows a thing or two already.

*You know them things out there? The …* and his words trailed off, but the Old Man didn't have to say any more. The Kid knew what he was talking about. Everybody knew what he was talking about.

At the mention, the Kid stood up tall, puffed up a little, the way all creatures do in moments like this. *Course I have. Just dealt with one the other night, in fact.* It was a well-practiced statement; no doubt the Kid had said something similar a couple, two, three times. With that old rifle slung on his back, and the way he stood and puffed himself up, who would think to argue?

*Must'a been something to see, that,* the Old Man replied, and the Kid stood down just as quick. He knew the Old Man wasn't like all those others, who didn't know, and were desperately afraid someone else did. They all listened, and nodded, and if they didn't believe the Kid they didn't dare say a word, because what if he was right after all? But the Old Man didn't suffer from any of that foolishness. He knew. And the Kid, to his credit, felt more than a little bit of embarrassment for even having said such a thing. He should'a known better.

The Old Man continued, not leaving the Kid to stew in that. *Well, whatever they are now, they used to be men. Still are, in a way.* Those words themselves cut right to the bone, and left the Kid with a chill. He knew the Old Man was right, though of course he had no way of knowing how he knew ... but that's how the Truth works. The Old Man just kept right on talking, *Make no mistake, kid, all the bad you see out there is the work of man. Careful not to forget that.* That last bit there, that was more of a command than a warning, and it sat hard on the Kid's ears.

It seemed like the Old Man had more to say, but his attention was caught by a glimmer of nothing, and he looked up, off, just past the Kid, who naturally had to turn and look himself. He followed the Old Man's eyes—he knew there weren't nothing but a wall there, but the way the Old Man looked, the way he focused, he might'a been looking ten miles past that wall. For all the Kid knew he could'a seen straightaways to that village the Kid was talking about, if'n it was even in the same direction as that. He might'a seen a thousand miles past, even, all the way to whatever was beyond that. Though the Kid sure as hell didn't see anything, and he was pretty damn certain the Old Man couldn't look through walls, he knew whatever the Old Man was seeing was different, and it definitely weren't good. Whatever it was, the Kid was disappointed he couldn't see it, because he would have liked to think he could help. He didn't say anything, partly because there wasn't much to say and partly because he was trying to remember his manners. And when he looked back—maybe with a mind to ask what the Old Man had seen—the Old Man already had a little nail in his hand. The Kid figured maybe it had come from somewhere under the bed, since he couldn't figure anywhere else it might'a come from, and the Old Man used it to carve a little cross in the wood of the floor, right there at the end of the blanket. Then the Old Man looked again, right back into that same spot that could'a been a thousand miles away—and damn it all if the Kid almost turned and looked again even though he knew there wasn't nothing there, so strong and focused was the way the Old Man looked—then the Old Man turned back and carved another little cross, just off to the side of the first, a little bigger this time.

The Kid couldn't help himself this time when he asked, *What are you doin' that for?* Which he didn't think was such a bad thing, since the Old Man had said hisself the curiosity wasn't harmful, and this did feel like something the Kid thought he should know, even if he was pretty sure he wouldn't have understood the answer, whatever it was gonna be.

*Bed's not perfect*, the Old Man said. It couldn't be called a response because he wasn't responding to what had been asked of him, he was just saying things. He said it as he brought himself to his knees, at the edge of the blanket on the floor, just like he'd always done before at the edge of the bed. *But it's better'n where you been sleeping on the road, I imagine.*

*Come on, now.* The Kid didn't need reminding of his manners for this. *I can't impose like that.* He meant it. He'd never meant anything more in his whole entire life. That just didn't seem right, coming into a man's house and taking what little he had, down to his bed, but the Old Man wasn't hearin' none of that fuss. He'd already bowed his head and closed his eyes.

*Night on the floor won't kill me*, the Old Man said, and then there was silence. A deep silence, as the Old Man prayed. The Kid didn't need to remember his manners to know there was nothing more to be said on the matter, and so he didn't.

## 4. The Darkest Part of the Night

THE OLD MAN AWOKE IN a cold sweat. Eyes wide open, though he didn't need to bother to look; he already knew: the Kid was gone. Bed'd been left made well as it could be, which said a lot about the Kid, given that the blanket wasn't much and there was nothing to rest a head on, and nothing fit right and none of that mattered much at all, but the Kid left it well as could be done none the same. Now, the Old Man knew he couldn't unmake a choice the way he could unmake a bed, so he lay back down on the floor, telling himself he was going back to sleep.

It comes as no surprise that was an empty lie, since the Old Man then found himself outdoors, long before sunrise, with a mind that he might as well start what passed for a day, now being as good as not now, since there was no point lying about whether he could ignore what happened and sleep. At least this way those rough hands wouldn't be left idle, and he could put off thinking every thought running through his mind for a little while longer. So he carried that same bucket filled with that same nothing over to that same trough … but there was something wrong. It wasn't that busted leg—the trough were still standing fine—it was something worse. Something that couldn't be set right on the uneven ground.

The pigs. He knew it was inevitable, as it is for all things, some sooner than others. He was still sad, because the Old Man felt like if nothing else, these pigs hadn't been given a fair shake; they'd been born into a world that wasn't fit for them, and they'd always done their best, as all the beasts under what passes for the sun do, but they'd started closer off to the end than felt right.

He went to check on them, just to be sure, since they deserved at least that much. One of them—that one, just there—was alive, even if barely. The Old Man went to her side and kneeled, checked on her as well as one can when they don't know exactly what they're checking for. *It's okay now, girl*, he said to her, *you just take it easy.* He offered her what succor words and a rough hand trying to be soft can give to a pig, which isn't much, so he added to that a handful of mash he brought close to her snout, and bless her little heart she ate up what little she could.

He stayed there by her side awhile, because that sweet girl deserved it, and he owed it to her—to all the pigs—to give them what little he could, since this world sure hadn't given them nothing worth a damn. He sat there by and by, and he stared out at that thunderstorm, and he looked off in the distance; that same long look he'd had the night before, and he thought … *Damn it, kid.*

Later, then, after a while of sitting with that pig, offering her what she would take and making sure she was as comfortable as he thought he could make her, he went out to the fallow with a shovel. The earth was hard—the Earth was hard, but he could only concern himself with what earth was here—and he got to digging. It took more than a few tries to get the shovel to catch through that hard earth, and under most circumstances a man would give up. But here, he owed the pigs something. It was a long time before he got that first hole dug, that first hole just about big enough for a pig.

THE THUNDERSTORM ARRIVED. EVEN AS the Old Man drove that old shovel into the hard earth, again and again, finishing those holes, finishing what he owed to the pigs, the sky got dark. Not dark the way it does when night comes, but the real dark, the dark when it should be light, that sends men packing inside to pray, with hopes this one isn't too bad. Lightning started, and it lit the Old Man's work … not that he would'a stopped on account of dark, mind you. He didn't need to see to know how big a hole needed to be to be fit for a pig. He kept on digging, even as thunder announced its arrival. Not a roar, like thunder sometimes has, but that low growl, the wave that a man can feel rattling his bones, like it's happening right inside him stead'a up in the sky.

No rain, though. Lightning enough to make the night seem day, and thunder enough to knock a mountain down, and still no rain. The Old Man looked off whence the storm came. All that time, all that time the storm hung in the distance, mocking the Old Man with its patience, he could at least tell hisself as bad as the storm was gonna be, whatever it brought with it, at least the damnable thing would also bring some rain. But it didn't. It brought terror, and it brought darkness, and it brought a heavy cloak onto his little patch of hard earth that he wasn't gonna stop digging in because he owed it to the pigs. It brought all those bad things, but it didn't think to bring any rain in exchange. The Old Man kept looking out whence the storm came … in the direction the Kid went.

Back inside the house, the Old Man knelt by the edge of his bed, but this time there were no prayers. His eyes were open, and he looked out, past the wall, way off in the distance whence the storm came, in the direction the Kid went. Coincidence, he hoped. Just a random trick that the Kid goes, and the storm comes, like the two couldn't occupy the same space. But the Old Man had been around a long time, a long time even before he ended up here, and he hadn't seen much that could be called coincidence. He had seen a lot of things happen that men wanted to say didn't have much to do with each other, but the Old Man knew better.

He got up, because he couldn't kneel here any longer. Not when the Kid had gone and that damn storm had come. If nothing else, he owed it to the pigs.

Out back, round the side of the old house, was the storm cellar. Well, the door to the storm cellar leastways—though that door was rotted through so much as to barely have earned calling itself a door. Sure enough, when the Old Man reached for that iron handle, it tore itself right off, along with half the rotted wood, and one of the hinges fell down into the cellar itself just to make the point that if the Old Man wanted the door to behave itself he should'a paid it a bit more mind back before this all happened. He promised he would come back and set things right—he owed the door to the storm cellar as well—but for the moment he needed to get down them stairs, which hopefully had held up a chance better than the door had.

Must'a taken some time for the Old Man to drag that ancient chest into the house, owing to how slow going these last couple feet was, and knowing he'd had to get it up the stairs that sure enough must have held up—better than the door, at least—under the weight. Satisfied, since where the chest was now was good as any place in this little house, the Old Man knelt—knelt in a different way than if he was going to pray, though in a way, this wasn't too different. He unhooked the first of the ancient locks; they was ornate, almost mystical things, the metal still strong even with a patina over it that could make you wonder if they'd outlived their usefulness. When he went for the second, the one that would'a rendered the chest open for a man to just reach in, he snatched his hand back. It was like the lightning outside had come and took a lash at him, and he pulled that hand back before the roll of thunder could follow up, and while it boiled and shook outside the Old Man just stared at the chest, stared at those locks.

He was back outside, standing by the ruined cellar door, a few rusted old tools in his hands. He wasn't examining the door like he should'a been, wasn't planning where the new planks needed to go, no. He was staring down, into the darkness of that cellar, where the chest had been. An eternity passed between the Old Man and the darkness, and even when the lightning whipped overhead as if to taunt the Old Man with a way to see down into that cellar, its light didn't pierce that darkness, and this time the Old Man didn't even hear the thunder. He couldn't quit thinking about that damn kid, and he couldn't quit thinking why the storm picked now of all times to bring its rails and booms, but didn't think to bring the rain with it. He knew none of this was a coincidence, and he knew he couldn't lie to himself and tell himself different, because no matter how much he tried he would know it wasn't the Truth, and that was something a man couldn't live with. So he left the tools, and he promised one day that cellar door would get fixed, but for the moment, he had to go back inside.

There, the Old Man paced, back and forth, back and forth, eyes on the chest. He would tear them away for a moment, to look at something—anything—else, but his eyes always went back to it. It was inevitable that he would look back, like it was inevitable he would eventually kneel afore it, inevitable he would open that chest, inevitable that he would reach inside. *Come for us all...* . he said to himself, as he finally did just that.

**AN OLD GUN BELT**, LIKE the kind a man with a wide-brimmed hat and dusty boots would wear hitched down a little on one side of his hip. He pulled that belt out, and sure enough, just as one would expect to find on that belt, knowing the kind of man who would wear it, a pair of twin revolvers sat in a pair of twin holsters. Both the handles of the revolvers—all that were visible—and the cracked leather of the holsters that hid the rest of those guns had unrecognizable letters tooled into them.

Unrecognizable because time and nature had taken their toll, or unrecognizable because the letters themselves didn't mean nothing to nobody anymore, well, that was impossible to figure.

The Old Man took that belt out and hooked it behind his back, caught that latch the first try, like the last time he'd done it was just yesterday. It fit perfect, hitched down a little bit on one side of his hip, exactly the way you'd expect a belt like that to be worn. The belt didn't change the way he moved at all, didn't take a second to get used to, and so nothing seemed all that different when the Old Man reached back down into the chest, for something that mattered even more.

A cross. Silver, seen through that muck that old metals get when they ain't stored right, and the moisture gets to 'em. It was rough and pitted, but that looked like a function of its making—not perfect, but made with care and caution and a mind to the work, which is the way things ought to be made. There was a leather cord, itself dry and cracked like the holsters, but that too was strung and tied with thoughtfulness and so it would be a while yet before it broke.

The Old Man held the cross in his hand, carefully, gently, and ran his thumb over the surface, tracing every pit and edge, each one bringing back a memory—some painful, like the scars, and some less painful, like something else. Satisfied with however many memories were stored in there, and whichever ones got brought to mind tracing it, he turned it over, revealing the large "M" etched into it, in a careful script made with a not-so-careful tool. He knew the letter was there, knew every curve of the script, but he had to look at it for a moment anyway, and he looked past the letter, through the cross, and off to another place and another time, and he saw the people and events that were there, all in his mind's eye, even if just for that moment.

The Old Man held that leather cord oh so carefully, even though he knew it wasn't about to break—not now; it wouldn't dare—and put it on over his head. It didn't weigh much more than nothing, but it pulled him down heavy, dragging him just that little bit lower and farther forward. He let it hang for a second before he had to take hold of it one more time, grip that silver tight now in his rough hands, digging it into the edges of his palm. That wasn't what caused the grimace, and that wasn't what caused the tears he was fighting back. In fact, holding on to that little thing for dear life may have been the only thing helping him fight back those tears at all.

A moment later he washed his face in that same bucket filled with the same stale water, by then the cross tucked under his shirt. Maybe so it wouldn't bang on things and get wet and a dozen other considerations, or maybe just because it was safer there, and that's where it belonged, really. And when the Old Man looked up, looked at that mirror, maybe it was because with all those other thoughts fighting for his attention he'd forgotten there weren't nothing to look back, its looking covered with that old fabric and the paper the Kid had tried his best to smooth back into its place. Or maybe he looked because he wondered, for the first time in a long time, if he shouldn't see what was under there.

He knew he shouldn't, like he knew so many other things ... but this, he had to. He shook a little as he pushed that fabric aside, making the motions like someone else was in control of his hand when he grabbed the edge of that paper. It was a good thing the Kid had already been at it; there was a fair enough chance if it was any more difficult than this, good sense would have gotten hold of the Old Man and he would have been able to stop himself. But this, being so easy, let him know it was the way it was supposed to be, and the thing he had to do. He closed his eyes, his hand moved as if in someone else's control, and maybe it was coincidence that just then a great booming thunder shook the very edges of creation, enough that he didn't hear the paper rip. And maybe too it was a coincidence when he finally opened those eyes, that a bolt of lightning like the sky itself tore asunder lit everything more than enough to see what the Old Man knew was waiting for him, why he'd covered that mirror all those years ago, and why he hadn't wanted to do any of this in the first damn place.

Whatever he saw there, just in that instant, almost before the sky had closed back up to the darkness again, he'd already turned away from, and gone out the door.

**THE PIG HADN'T MOVED MUCH.** Not that there was anywhere else it would go, even if it could. By now, her breathing was shallow, though it seemed what little succor was brought to her earlier had helped, in as much as those things can. Her ears perked, just before the Old Man appeared again at her side—this time he had two buckets, which came as quite a surprise for this sweet girl who hadn't known what a surprise was and certainly never had the chance to have one. He laid one on its side, close to her. He stood the other one up, close enough.

*Eat that one*, he said to her. Not quite a command but a gentle suggestion, though one that both parties knew ought to be taken seriously. *If ye get strong enough, eat this one.* The pig, of course, didn't understand, but the words still meant something. *If ye don't, won't matter.* He balanced those ungentle words with a gentle pat, as gentle as rough hands could manage, since he owed her at least that much.

With that, he started walking. He stopped when he got to the fence—that old, rotted idea of a barrier that couldn't keep nothing out, if even there was anything that wanted in—and he turned back to the pig. *More in the trough*, he let her know. *And if that corn ever come up outta there, well, I guess you can just have that too.* He continued walking, now, and the pig watched him just a moment, since it was dark and she couldn't see much. More to the point, that food was close, spilling as it was from the bucket on the ground, and she knew that she would have to get to it soon if there was gonna be any getting to it … especially as the first drops of rain started then to hit the ground.

**OUT HERE, THINGS WERE DIFFERENT.** Far from the death and emptiness that surrounded the Old Man, this was lush, green, and alive. The sun shone. Nature had long since reclaimed what man had once abandoned.

Was there someone left who remembered the names of the plants, of the mosses and lichens, of the sprouting mushrooms and crawling vines and climbing ivies?

Did it matter?

## 5. A Mountain Pass

**IT WAS ANOTHER OF MANY nights** since the one when the Kid had left the Old Man's house and set out his own way. What set things apart tonight was the Kid had found himself on and in between a row of rocky walls, a thousand crags fighting amongst themselves, where he'd come upon a place to make a camp. It was as good a place as any, and the best place he'd been in some time, save for the few hours he'd been at the homestead. It was dark, as there was no moon, and so he kept his fire low, the way he'd always been taught.

The Kid had his old radio with him. It was special to him, not simply because few people had one, but because he knew fewer still could do what futzing and jury-rigging it took to keep such a thing working. This was one of those things what took more than its fair share of know-how, and the Kid let himself have a bit of pride in the fact that he'd had enough for this.

At this moment though, it seemed the share he had weren't quite enough, as all it let him hear was static, even when he made those small adjustments he'd taught himself, after he'd first learned what others could teach. Moments like that lead to frustration, and frustration oftentimes leads to mistakes, so the Kid remembered his manners—manners he'd been taught even when it was just him, since it was good to treat oneself well, as he'd heard said—and moved the dial oh so slowly to try and find more than the hisses and pops it offered now. A good thing that the Kid remembered those manners, fought the frustration, and moved cautiously from nothing to a crackle then back to nothing again, because in one of the nothings he heard a noise— not from the radio, but from somewhere else. Somewhere close by enough that he could hear it, which meant that somewhere close by could hear him too.

The Kid moved quick—not as quick as the Old Man had moved, when they'd first met, but the Kid thought maybe that might'a been a trick or maybe the Kid looked away or maybe there was a score of other reasons— the Kid could move quick enough, and as fast as another man would have to stop and think of what to do, the radio was already off and the fire already out, kicked over with dirt from the mound the Kid was always taught to keep nearby for moments such as this. He added to the silence with his own practiced kind of quiet, where everything in the body but the eyes and ears shut off.

That meant the Kid ignored the smell of the burnt embers, and the taste of what little he'd had to eat left on his tongue, but he did remember hearing some time back that everything was in fact a form of touch—the sounds was just touching your ears and even the light just touching your eyes, though there weren't no light to speak of since the fire was gone—and the Kid stopped himself from thinking such thoughts, remembering there was a noise, and if that noise touched his ears again something else might just up and touch him if he didn't see to them first.

There's a rhythm to quiet. And rhythm is a funny thing—another sense, in a way—wherein it can't be taught; y'either have it or you don't. There's a natural ebb and lap, a flow, a time of quiet, and then times in between the quiet—not noise, something far from it—but moments where the quiet don't matter so much. Where it ain't so ... quiet. Those are the moments when the Kid moved. Slow but fast, knew where to put his feet so he wouldn't slide or kick up dust, where the rocks and packed ground and roots would hold him just fine, and let him up just near the top of one of those rocks, where he could get a good look around. There was still no moon, and no light was touching his eyes, but it was still better to be up high. If things couldn't see him, at least he'd have a better spot from which he couldn't see them neither.

Up top, right as he got up there, right as that flow waned and the quiet part of the quiet started up again, there was another noise. It was two of them now, distinct and different as far as he could tell, as though the valleys and passes and crags were playing tricks on his ears, and it weren't easy to feel where either sound was touching him from. He listened hard, begged his eyes to work just a little harder, to reach out and feel for what light there was, to no avail. He stayed up there, listening, long enough, before the quiet waxed and he took the moment to head back down toward his camp. Leastways, he could gather what meager things he had and move along, or move somewhere else, or ...

He caught sight of the camp, a dying glow from a handful of embers touching his eyes just enough. What he saw touched those hairs on the back of his neck, tightened that skin into gooseflesh, and before he knew it that rifle was slung round into his hands.

The radio was gone. While it had most certainly happened, in the Kid's mind it still stood as impossible, since there wasn't a hint of a noise from down here even during the unquiet parts of the quiet, and even then neither of the noises was from behind him in the first place.

*Who's out there?* he called, trying to puff himself up like creatures big and small do, but the words caught and cracked in his throat when they came out. And maybe that's why whatever was behind him thought it was then okay to take a step closer and reach out for him.

By the time the Kid spun round, quick as a whip, and brought that rifle up the way he'd practiced a thousand times, to have it ready on just about anything of any size, it was gone. There was nothing, where a moment before he was sure there'd been something. And whatever it was most certainly didn't get outta sight—what little sight there could be with no light to touch your eyes—because nothing could be first there and then so soon after not there, not as quick as the Kid could, and had, turned round with his rifle.

Behind him—again—there was movement. A different kind of movement now; not a fast, creeping up kinda movement, but the frantic, scrabbling movement of running away. No regard for the noise, as the quiet had long been abandoned; now it just went.

*Hey! Hey, stop!* the Kid called. And while he knew that was futile, just like calling out the first time had been, it was the kind of thing that was done in a time like this. And the thought that whoever—though it could have been a whatever—might have had that radio, well, the Kid couldn't let that just go. He gave a reckless chase, this time not paying much mind to where his feet landed or how much rock or dust kicked up. Now, it was about catching up and getting that radio. Never mind whoever—whatever—might not have the know-how, and the thing might be useless to them.... That would be even worse. Then the Kid would'a lost something and whoever—whatever—would have gained nothing.

It was difficult to run with the rifle in his hands, stead'a slung over his back like he was used to—he was used to bringing the rifle round only when it was time to use it, not when he was looking for the chance—and maybe it was that, and maybe it was the fact that he wasn't paying attention to where his feet were going, and maybe it was because he didn't stop to take stock of the quiet because there wasn't time for that just right this second, but the Kid didn't notice that there was someone else—something else—following him.

Just as that who or what was about to catch up with him, the fact that the Kid—who didn't think to be careful about such things—wasn't paying attention to where his feet were landing finally caught up with him. He landed just sideways on a patch of loose rock, and those things all gave way at the same time, and what felt like a whole mountain of scree and man and rifle slid down in a heap, all at once. It wasn't a long fall, though the Kid didn't have time to be thankful for that right at this very minute.

Above him, from the rocks—of course the part of the rocks that stood firm and didn't send a body down after him—something watched. It wasn't that any more light touched its eyes than did the Kid's, it was more like it needed less light, or maybe better knew the difference in the patches of darkness, for this was its natural habitat. Whatever the reason, it watched the Kid as he stood up, and though the Kid looked right back whence he fell, right to the rock where it was standing, for whatever the reason, whatever it was didn't touch his eyes.

So the Kid got to his feet, quick as he could manage. Had the rifle at the ready, for no good reason at all, really, since no light touched his eyes at all now. The real dread and worry crept in now, the knowledge from experience that a step in the wrong direction meant a fall, and the dice might not roll his way a second time. Only then might he be thankful for that first fall to have not been so short, since then that second one might be.

HE HEARD A GUNSHOT. Instinct pulled him down and into himself just a little, as though that would have made a difference. Once instinct let go and his mind was allowed to think and be and know things again, the first thing he knew was that shot most certainly wasn't his, since he knew for absolute certain he hadn't fired his rifle; if he had, instinct wouldn't have taken hold like it did. Besides, this sounded ... different. That shot rang clear and true, and all at once set the rocks and mountains and hills awash in vibration that touched the Kid's ears in just the right way, so that he knew exactly where all of them were. The Kid kept the rest of his instinct at bay—instinct that wouldn't serve him well right now—and listened, scanning the rocks he now knew the locations of, waiting. And when the quiet ebbed, as quiets do, patience paid off like it does for a fisherman when he knows there's something in the reeds, even if it ain't biting just this minute. The Kid finally heard the sound of someone—something—moving. He moved, too. A slow, stalking movement, keeping pace, remembering the way the vibrations touched his ears, knowing where the rocks were, where his feet could go. So cautious were his movements, so linked with the quiet, so focused was he on knowing where the rocks were and where his foot could go, the Kid still didn't notice there was another him—another someone, or something—following. As he stalked, it stalked, on the ground, behind him. Each footstep the same, each calm breath—fighting off instinct—the same.

Weren't long before the rocks and hills and mountains opened up, and the Kid found hisself in a clearing. His first thought was to wonder why he didn't push on just a little farther, earlier in the night, and make his camp here, rather than amongst the crags where his feet would slip. His second thought was of what he saw now, since what little light there was deigned to touch his eyes, and his second-and-a-half thought, as close to instinct as one could come, was to bring that rifle up to his cheek, the way he'd been taught and practiced a thousand times. Because there, near the rocks, just across the open and flat little place that would have been so nice to make a camp, was a body.

Hard to make out many details at this distance, but the one detail that could be made was the most important of 'em, because that detail was this body was dead, and that meant most of the other pressing details—the wheres and whys and whatfors—weren't all that important right in this moment. The Kid lowered the rifle, as rifles and their ilk were only good for one thing, and that one thing had already been done in this instance, so the Kid didn't think it was gonna serve much purpose for the next little moment. He started to get closer, with a mind to be cautious at first—but the same way instinct takes over and makes a man do a thing that won't necessarily make much difference in a situation, something else took over him now. The Kid never-minded caution, didn't bother to watch where his feet were going. He dropped the rifle, his only thought and concern in the world to get closer to that body.

At the same time, off and over to the side of the little flat clearing, what light there was touched a set of eyes. Those eyes watched, and followed the Kid, and as the Kid got closer to the edge of the clearing where he saw that body, the eyes got closer to him. Those eyes didn't bother to match their steps or watch where their feet went, since they knew the Kid weren't gonna notice, focused as he was. And once the Kid was close enough to make out many of the details, well … that was the moment he wished a different kind'a instinct would'a took over, and made him turn and run, flailing, yelling like a madman, and never come back. For when the Kid knelt down near the body, he saw what it was.

It was the Kid. He was sure of it. It was the same face he'd seen in that reflection, all those nights ago. Dirty, with deeper lines than he'd remembered, even though it'd been a while since he'd seen it before that last time, so the more of anything seemed to make sense. There was a mole, the one he'd had since he was a real and proper kid, right there, on its lip. Reflex—a cousin of instinct, more useful in certain moments—made the Kid reach up and touch his own; right there, same place. It couldn't be, he thought, but that didn't matter in the face of things that was. And though he knew, he had to know. So the Kid reached out, slowly, terrified, doing a thing he shouldn't, but felt compelled to anyway, just so he could know.

THE KID AWOKE IN DARKNESS. Seemed that each of his senses would take their own sweet time to come around; his ears were touched first, by a sound he couldn't quite place, even though he knew he recognized it. It was tapping, that part was for sure. Not quite rhythmic, but forced, alternating…. He knew that sound. Even before any of the other senses saw it to wake up, a thought touched his mind—that was flint, hitting steel. Maybe the other way round, but he knew the sound.

Funny, how the order of things go sometimes. The Kid knew that sound, knew what must be happening, long before his body knew it was touching the ground, or that the dull spice of dirt touched his tongue, or his eyes finally decided it was time they opened, so he could find out just what the hell was going on. He was at his camp. He—it—back at the same place they'd been. Back, too, was the radio, though there was no telling what state it was in, since it wasn't even giving off the little bits of static…. Maybe it just needed a little know-how. The Kid thought about what might need'n to be done to it, and he thought to hisself again how funny it was to consider such things when he didn't have any real clue just what the hell was going on.

The Old Man was there, too. Not back, since he hadn't been there previous, but there in the way that certain folk always just seem to belong, wherever they are. It was the Old Man working that flint and steel—or steel and flint, maybe—and little sparks and glints touched the Kid's eyes, and he saw the Old Man might'a been bordering up toward a legitimate emotion for the first time … least the first time the Kid had seen.

*Why'd you put out the fire?* the Old Man muttered, and the Kid was certain now: that was frustration. It was a relief, in a way; the Kid could tell himself the Old Man was a man after all, like any other man with a damnable piece of flint and steel where each weren't working the way he wanted, where a situation like that could cause at least some kind of reaction.

The Kid thought again how funny it was that thoughts like that would streak through and touch his mind first, before he even thought to ask, *What are you doing here?* Which was a much more sensible thing to want to know, rather than whether the Old Man could get frustrated or not.

*Tryin' to get this lit, so we don't freeze to death.* And the Old Man must'a noticed the way he'd spoken before, because this response was cold and dead and matter-of-fact and free of any of those feelings. It was back to just the way things was.

*Who was that?* The Kid knew they was having two different conversations again, but he was ready for it, this time. The Old Man had got the drop on him when they'd first met, when the Kid was expecting something different, so he'd stuttered and stammered and minded his manners; now, he knew better. What's more, the Old Man knew he knew better.

*Thought you had all the answers?* the Old Man sorta coughed out, as he kept on with his work.

*Was it one of them?* The Kid was almost excited by the thought, forgetting that previously he might'a let on that he'd seen one of 'em before, even though he knew the Old Man knew better. And before the Kid could insist that the Old Man answer, with that kinda pause that lets another man know he expected it to be filled, the Kid remembered, *It looked like me.* That memory came rushing back and hit him like a heavy boot on the chest.

*Yeah, they do that.* The Old Man got struck by his own memory, by a score of 'em, maybe. But before they could do those things memories do, especially when they're unwanted and they hit you in the chest like a heavy boot, he went back to striking that damn steel and flint.

Still nothing, but that frustration at least gave the Kid time to come around proper. More thoughts and memories started to come back and take root in his mind, and he forced himself up with an elbow.... . *Careful. Might wanna take it slower than that,* the Old Man warned him. And before the Kid could embarrass himself by arguing, everything went dark again for what felt like more than a second. Even though the light from the sparks was still touching his eyes, everything else wasn't doing its job right, and the Kid took hisself a deep breath and thought maybe this time he might listen.

*Did you see what happened?* Now the Kid's hand started searching about, almost on its own, for the source of a nagging feeling he couldn't quite put a name to yet.

*You were gonna touch it,* the Old Man started—for a second there, the Kid thought he might'a been talking about where his hand was searching now, and then he chided himself for not following along quick enough, as the Old Man continued, *I had to stop ye.* It's like the words were punctuated by the Kid's hand, as it found the source of that nag: a split, with a bit of swelling and some dried blood, all on the back of his head.

Now, he'd had a scrape or two in his life—this was a hard world after all and a man, even a kid, wasn't gonna get out unscathed— but this was something different, even he knew that. *You hit me?* the Kid realized; he said it almost to himself, rather than to the Old Man, like an accusation. And followed up with, *Why?* which the Kid thought was a reasonable enough question.

So it came as quite a shock to him when the Old Man tossed that damnable flint and steel down and what was once just a spark of frustration flared up into a proper fire of sorts, skipping all the in-between parts, and he more spit the words than spoke 'em, *So you wouldn't touch it! Now damn it, kid, why'd you put out this fire?*

The Old Man knew it wasn't right, the way he was acting nor the way he was feeling, so he stood up and off to the side. The Kid thought to himself the Old Man hadn't forgotten his manners neither, since he hisself was always taught to go stand off to a side and get a deep breath when those kinda fires flared up as well. And though the Old Man wasn't looking at him, exactly, the Kid still held up a hand as a way to apologize—now, it wasn't his fault exactly that the Old Man was feeling how he was feeling, since no man controls another man's thoughts, but the Kid didn't want the Old Man to think he was antagonizing, and besides, the reasons didn't matter if you wanted a result.

Since everything was working together right by now, the Kid was able to bring himself up to something like a crouch without losing his balance or worrying about things going back to darkness. He took his pack—that was close by enough, just like it was before—and felt around inside as he talked, and this time made sure to lighten his tone, and speak soft, so's the Old Man would know he didn't mean no harm. *So it couldn't see me,* the Kid explained. *First thing they teach you.*

And since the Old Man had taken that breath, he came in closer to the fire again and stood over it when he said, *Learnin' from the wrong people, then. Fire itself ain't the problem. It's the standin' near fire that gets you in trouble.* And like it was gonna make any bit of difference, he stoked the dry, lifeless kindling with a boot. *Fire's like bait in a trap. Draws 'em in, holds 'em there.* But there was no fire now, and no amount of boot-stoking was gonna change that.

The Kid, still digging around in the pack—his hands hadn't touched the right thing, hadn't felt the right shape in the right pouch yet—nodded at his rifle, off to the side there, just within reach. Exactly where it should'a been. *I would have been fine,* he said. He meant it, too.

*And what were you planning to do about the other ones?* the Old Man asked, no hint of emotion behind those words. Just a question, even if he didn't really need to know the answer.

*What other ones?*

The answer might not have come as a surprise to the Old Man, but the question had definitely come as a surprise to the Kid. *Exactly*, the Old Man said, finally, though they both knew he didn't need to.

By now, the Kid had found it. The right shape in the right pouch touched the Kid's hands, and he pulled it out of his pack, proud. Proud both that he had found it, and proud of the thing itself: a lighter; old and metal, well used and cherished. The Kid held it up to his ear and shook it, and the sounds he was hoping for touched his ear: should be enough left.

*Did you think you were shooting at me?* the Kid asked as he made his way to the kindling, not really bothering to stand up all the way so's the whole motion was a bit more awkward than he would have liked it to be, what with only having one hand to balance on the ground since he had the lighter in the other.

*Why would I think that?* the Old Man asked, and this time it was a question that he really did need to know the answer to. He'd known the reality of things for so long, it was so ingrained and such a part of him, that he forgot other people might not know it yet.

*Because he looked just like me*, the Kid said, at the same time as he lit that fire. The Old Man was just starting to say something, but in that wane of quiet the fire caught, quick as that. No striking flint on steel—not by hand leastways—before the kindling caught, and in that first flash of ember maybe, just maybe, the Old Man recoiled just a bit. Maybe it was a trick of the light and shadow, but maybe if you'd got to watch that same moment a hundred times over, you might pick up just the slightest cinch in the face, a twitch that tightened one of those scars, and you might worry to yourself it looked a little like fear. Maybe not fear of something that was gonna happen, but maybe fear of something that already had.

But the moment was gone as soon as it come, and without a hundred times to watch it the Kid was none the wiser. His pride in getting that fire lit more than took up his attention, enough that he didn't even know the Old Man had stopped short from saying something at first. So when the Old Man finally did say, *Only to you. I can tell the difference,* that just seemed like the natural continuation of the conversation.

*Difference between what?* the Kid asked, earnest again. If'n even he was planning to put on airs about what he knew or didn't at some point in the future, he wasn't doing it now.

*I knew it wasn't you.* The Old Man had that habit of saying things in a way that sounded like he thought it answered everything. But even the Kid knew answers like that often left a man with more questions than he had before.

The Kid looked around the campsite, tried to get his bearings. He had no idea where the sound had come from, where he'd gone, where he'd fell, no idea where the clearing was. The whole thing could'a happened a world away or right next to him and he wouldn't'a known the difference. *Where is he? I want to see him,* he finally said.

*You already did.* There it was again, like the Old Man thought that answered everything.

The Kid had had enough; questions were pushing through his head and none of them seemed like they shouldn't be answered, seeing as they all had to do directly with him. *I want to know what happened.*

The Old Man knew he meant it, and he thought for a while there, and he figured to himself maybe the Kid deserved to know, after all. He spoke slow, deliberate; even more so than usual. *It was after you. Now it's not. It's buried, in the ground, where it should be*. And the Old Man answered the next question too, before the Kid even had a chance to ask it. *One shot, straight through the heart. All you need to know about dealing with them.*

The Kid let the Old Man's words do their work in his mind, all's he had to do was let them until he truly understood. And while he did so, the Old Man scraped out a little patch of dirt on the ground, moved the rocks and detritus, until it was about the size of a bed. *I told you to go home, and ye didn't listen. And then that thing is out there, and it's following you, and ye got no idea. And you put out yer fire, and you get close enough to almost touch it, and …* Even the Old Man didn't want to consider the words he would have had to say next. This time, he didn't have to. Even if the Kid didn't know, he knew.

*Why you doing this, kid? Why's it gotta be you?*

It was a hell of a question, and the Kid was quiet for a second, as this time the memory didn't come like a bullet but like a butterfly, tossing and flittin' out around the side of his vision, something beautiful and natural, something that even if you never get a right look at it, you know it was special, and you were just happy it was there. He let that memory run its course, smiled, and spoke clear and low.

*She would sit up late, when she still could, and tell me stories. Stories of great men, of the sacrifices they made … of the great things that came of those sacrifices.* The memories continued. A flood, now, of the most magnificent and wondrous creatures under the sky. The Kid kept his eyes closed this time, sitting amongst their glory.

*She said for even the least likely of us there was a great thing, just waiting. Something for them to become, if they had the faith to see it through.* Tears, now. The kind no man worries after, no man is ashamed of, because no man in the world doesn't know the source, and wouldn't feel the same.

*She said I could stop Him. That my death would be His undoing.* The Kid's tears stopped, and his eyes opened. In them now burned the fire of Truth. He wiped the last of the tears from his cheek, since the moment had passed and now he caught himself worrying about the thoughts and concerns of others, and felt a twinge embarrassed. It was reasonable, to be sure, but he needn't have worried about that, not in the presence of the Old Man. He who was one of the only left who could understand.

*… But you aim to save yourself by killing Him, instead.* Understand he did.

The Kid heard those words from the Old Man and the tears started again; not from the glory, but from the anger and frustration of a thing that just isn't fair. *How can you ask that of someone?* the Kid almost howled. *It's not fair to place that burden on another's shoulders.*

Truth is no different than water and air; it don't mean nothing, don't want nothing. It simply is. But Truth so often feels personal, or wrong, or evil, like it has a mind of its own. The Old Man knew that as well as anyone. But he had come to terms with his Truth—his and so many others—a long, long time ago. So it was just as well he could now meet this Truth, the Kid's, with serenity and acceptance.

*No. I don't suppose it is. Ye gotta take it on of your own free will. Otherwise, it's too daunting a thing, to know what's waiting for you, and for others to ask ye to press on anyway.* The Old Man spoke with a measure of care, and concern, and enough understanding that the Kid knew it wasn't cold comfort, but instead came from a genuine place.

The Kid hadn't noticed before, lost as he was in the Truth, but the Old Man had finished with that little patch of ground and had switched to lashing those bits of detritus together, wood and rock and any old thing, and had made crosses. Only a few, and some more the idea of a cross than anything, but the Old Man planted them in the ground just the same.

*Is it safe here, then?* the Kid asked, and he realized it was one of those questions he'd wanted to know the answer to for a while now but hadn't gotten around to asking yet. *Will that protect us? Keep them out?*

The Old Man kneeled, not even needing to be careful to avoid the crosses—he knew where they were. And he knew that was another one of those questions didn't need an answer; the Kid would figure it out on his own if he put a mind to it. So he answered a different question. One the Kid hadn't asked, and probably never would have known to ask, until it was too late. *Be thankful you only see a reflection, kid. Pray you never see nothing else. Pray you never see what they really look like.* The Old Man then bowed his head, poetically, in prayer, and wasn't about to say no more.

The Kid was left trembling; not out of cold, for the fire took and burned well, and would provide all the heat they'd need for the night. No, here he trembled for everything else there was, and there were no flames in the world able to fight those concerns back. So instead, his hand found a pocket, and inside felt the shape of a flask, which he took out and flicked open in a practiced move that he fancied himself a good hand at, and then took a quick sip. It was the kind of thing other men told him would help, even though they themselves may have been pretending, but he'd tried it anyway because he didn't know any better and there wasn't a thing else he could think of trying.

IT WAS A FITFUL WAY of sleeping, so much so it almost wasn't fair to call it sleep. The Kid never got laying down right. His arm was always in the wrong spot, that patch on the back of his head would come with a twinge of pain at just the wrong moment, right before he thought he was done with all the bother, and start everything up again. So when that deep, rumbling boom hit, somewhere way off in the distance, it didn't make much difference to the Kid, seeing as how he was halfway between sleep and wake the whole time anyway, so the one didn't make too much difference over th'other.

He sat right up. This wasn't no slow-going, one-thing-touch-your-mind-at-a-time nonsense now; this was that state where every part of a man was reaching out past its limits to feel for what there was to know about what'd just happened, so's he could up and at 'em with the best plan of action in the shortest time. The Kid didn't have to look round to know the Old Man was up as well. 'Sat thunder? the Kid asked him, and it was more hopeful than it was an honest guess, 'cause even if he'd never heard a thing like it in his life, he sure as hell knew what it wasn't.

It sounded again, as though it was trying to answer for itself, to reach out to the Kid and tell him no, no in fact it weren't thunder. Thunder was something a man would face innumerable times, oftentimes welcome, other times a nuisance, but always natural. Always a part of the world. Even a thunder like what come with the storm to the old homestead, as unnatural and mean-spirited as that storm felt, at least it was a part of the world. This, though … this weren't nothing a man should ever have to face. This was something so much worse than "worse," there weren't yet a name for it.

Nothin' to concern yourself with, the Old Man finally replied, after the sound had cleared out of the air around them, and things were quiet again. And while that weren't exactly a lie, it also weren't exactly the truth, and more so it weren't nothin' the Kid was gonna listen to either way. He was up quick, started collectin' his things. Focused. Utterly focused. Waiting for that noise again, almost hopeful.... *What if it's Him?*

*All the more reason,* the Old Man replied, but he knew the Kid wasn't gonna listen—mostly on account'a the Kid wasn't listening—and before the Old Man's words were even all the way out the Kid was up, and the rifle was slung across'd his back so he could move quicker than when it was in his hands, and he was headed off toward the direction of the sound. There wasn't nothing specific about the direction and there didn't need to be, because everywhere in a whole general area was in the direction of the sound.

The Old Man watched him go, watched that figure recede into the dust and into the distance. Watched him just awhile, and his face cinched and those scars tightened and there was a glimmer of disappointment, which itself was tempered by the tide of understanding. The Old Man had been a kid once, a Kid once, too, and what kinda man would he have become if he'd'a listened and not gone to see for hisself what that damnable sound was, and if there was something he could do to help? So the Old Man stood up, and he too would'a collected his things, but he didn't have much to collect. The belt he was still wearing—he slept in that well enough—and the cross was safe under his shirt where it would stay. He didn't need nothin' else ... but the Kid might, and the Old Man knew he couldn't let the Kid go it alone, and so he followed.

## 6. Halfway Between the City and Nowhere

IT WAS FARTHER THAN THE Kid thought, however far he thought it was gonna be. By now he was exhausted, as he'd been going at it hard the better part of the day. He had figured wherever he was going couldn't'a been that far off, owin' as to how damn loud the thing was ... but the harsh realities of time and distance he was facin' now let him know he clearly wasn't much for figuring. He finally stopped to rest for a bit, had to pull a slug of water out of his old canteen. He always made sure to fill it with fresh water every chance he got, but still made sure to save enough just in case. He drank and caught his breath, and he cursed himself—even though it wasn't specifically his fault— that he hadn't gotten any real rest the night before.

The Kid looked back the direction he came, and shook his head just a little. It wasn't from surprise, because if you'd put the question to him he would'a guessed this would happen, but it was more from a sense of accepting the fact that the Old Man was following him. Granted, it could have been any figure making its way, steady like it was, through that haze of heat burning off the ground ... but in this case the Kid was pretty confident in his way of figuring. And maybe it was good luck, that he had looked back at the Old Man just then. It could have also just been the way things work out exactly the way they're supposed to—mostly owing to the fact that things can only work out that one way, which is the way they did. There was no use to the Kid, or anyone, really, worrying about how things would'a been different ... since if one thing was different, so was all things, and worrying about how if a leaf would'a fallen left instead'a right had about as much to do with reality as wondering what would'a happened had he been looking forward instead'a back.

Because at that moment, the way things were, the Kid was looking back toward where the Old Man was coming, steady like it was, instead of forward, to where a bright flash'a light suddenly took over the ground and sky and everything in between, and shine't brighter than the sun when the sun was shining proper, and not through a gray pallor as it mostly did these days.

That flash was everything, all in an instant, and there was no telling where it came from nor how far away it was, because it was everywhere all at once. As soon as that light withdrew and the Kid knew it was safe to open his eyes and look forward again—he wasn't sure when he'd closed his eyes, only that he must have, since he'd opened them again—he took off. He ran reckless, a while still, made more a while by the fact he was still exhausted and hadn't refilled the canteen, but none of that mattered because he needed to reach the source, to see for himself. He ran, ignoring the burn and ache of running, not even forcing his legs to move, simply ignoring the fact they wanted to stop. He ran, until there were no other ways to describe it, and didn't slow up until he saw that first body.

It was lying in a field, near a granary. The building had long since been abandoned and even longer since been maintained, but as was true of a rifle, there was no mistaking what it had once been for. Even in death, even no longer capable of serving its purpose, it still was that thing. Like the body, in a way, the Kid supposed. It didn't stop being a man just 'cause it weren't breathing.

The Kid wasn't sure why he got closer, just that he felt he should. It wasn't until he got close enough—close enough to see that it was stiff and cold, a body long since dead, whether you knew a thing about bodies or not—that he understood his need to get close and look was to make sure it didn't look like him. Sure enough, the face wasn't the same, even without the fact that mushrooms had taken root—or whatever mushrooms took to start themselves—and were growing out through the eyes. Satisfied—not in the fate of the man, of course, simply that the man looked like hisself, stead'a like the Kid—the Kid kept on through the field. Things only got worse, as there were more bodies. More bodies. More. None of them looked like the Kid, as far as the Kid could see. And there was whole fields, burned. Farmers too. Where wheat should be blowing gently in a breeze—there was a breeze, now; and strange as it may seem the absence of anything blowing in it was the only reason the Kid noticed—there was nothing. Scorched marks where there should have been crops, scorched marks where there had once been men. They were all arranged haphazard; maybe a macabre pattern if you'd seen it from up high enough, but from here, on the ground, there was no meaning. No pattern. No reason. There was only the bodies, and what had once been wheat.

The Kid had kept walking, trying to care enough to take each one in, but after a while they all just become one. It was just death, rather than someone died. There weren't no single man or woman or child, there was only bodies. He was left awash in occhiol—something more or less than a sorrow, simply an understanding of one's place, one's smallness, in the entirety of creation. It wasn't until he reached the edge of a hill, that the occhiol was replaced with sonder, as the Kid was suddenly struck with the greatness and understanding of something he—like everyone—had always known, but no one had necessarily made words for yet, so's he couldn't quite put a finger on the thing he felt. It was then he began to truly understand that each and every being—every man and child he'd ever passed—living or dead—every woman he'd heard a story about, every being great and small—was their own living and breathing creature, part of a life as full and complete and wondrous as his own. Each individual he'd ever tipped his hat to across the way, that same one had gone on to do their own things, live in their own world, play out the role they was given. Each of us meant everything, to ourselves. And we was each the whole of the entirety of our own creation. In a moment, the two of them great and powerful feelings clashed hard inside the Kid's mind, breaking waves of knowledge that he—the Kid—meant only as much or as little as each of those folks had ever meant to him … and to most, nothing at all. Nothing. Utter, un-contemplative, un-understandable, nothing. He, like everyone, had little, and meant less, and ultimately all would return to dust, and the soil would turn over, and in a time none would remember any of the others, and that was just the same as never having existed in the first place.

When such a wave breaks in a man's mind, and the current pulls on his every little thought, it tends to leave him standing still, staring out at what he now truly understood as nothing. And this was just how the Old Man found the Kid, when he finally caught up, in his own time. And you could excuse the Old Man for not knowing that wave had crashed, that instead thinking the Kid was seeing the truth and reality of just what he saw below, and not understanding the entirety of all creation and his place within it in that moment there. Truth be told, what the Old Man saw would have rendered him the same, struck him dumb and almost blind, were he to come across'd it as the Kid had done.

IT WAS ONCE A SMALL settlement, abutting the bank of a river. Modest: a mill and a few houses, some more permanent than others, but it was beginning to expand. Soon it became large enough to attract people, some from far away, seeking something better than what they'd had at home.

All would be welcome. For if the mill was staffed, if the farmers had all the hands they'd want in the fields, perhaps a small shop could be opened to satisfy some need that had gone unfulfilled to that point. So the town would grow, like all of them do. So would the people there have a little place of this world to call their own, to be proud of, and hope that perhaps they could leave something behind for their children, so those lives could be better than their parents' had been.

Now, though? It would be remembered only as the site of a battle. Not a great battle, as the histories and legends of those things were measured, but a battle great enough to those people of the mill.

The dead numbered in the dozens, strewn about chaotically, no easily perceived flow or logic to it all. To a practiced eye, it was clearly less a fight than a massacre; fierce, though, and brutal, and none of the slain lay in peace. Bodies were sundered, faces twisted into grotesque masks. To walk among them would be to feel the same anguish, pain, and terror, such as they must have felt in their final moments.

It is a terrible thing to consider, this staggering loss of life. How can a heart go untroubled, knowing that each of the dead is— was—a part of something greater, now missing from the world, never to be regained or recovered? For once one thing was changed, everything was different. The world would never be the same.

*Come on, then.* The Kid barely had time to hear the Old Man's words before an iron grip had him fast, and led him down the hill, toward it all. Even if the Kid had the wherewithal to think to pull free, to set his feet against the slide and choose for himself where he wanted to go, there was no choice whether the Old Man's hand stayed firm to his arm. Before the Kid could object, even if that was what he would have done, they were in the carnage, the charred ground cracking and giving way like old, rotted wood beneath their boots.

There was wreckage of old machines. Metal and bodies were both twisted. The only thing alive—not *left* alive, no, for nothing survived this—the only thing alive were the flies, and only because they had come later. And so the Kid and the Old Man were like flies, too, having come later, to buzz and dart their way through this nightmare. And for what? Perhaps the answer lay in the barracks—or, that is, what was left of what likely was a barracks—which is where the Old Man pulled the Kid, forcing him into and amongst what were likely once workers, now dead in what were likely once their beds. There were more than a few cots left empty, though no less affected by what had ruined everything else, and the Old Man shoved the Kid towards one, then nodded. And when the Kid looked, first at what was once a cot, and then back to the Old Man—he couldn't believe that the Old Man meant what it seemed he meant by this gesture—the Old Man nodded again.

*You can't be serious,* and the Kid meant it. But the Old Man pulled the Kid's pack down, rough, and tossed it down by what was once a cot. There were no gentleness left in the hands, only the roughness.

There was roughness in the voice, too, as the Old Man spoke. *No point pressin' on any further. Not yet.*

*I ain't sleeping here,* the Kid responded, and he damn well meant it. He was a man, too, and he wasn't about to let the Old Man treat him in such a way. He was trembling, being so close to so much death as he was, and all the waves that had broken over him earlier reminding him they was still there, that they hadn't been fully dealt with yet neither.

*Y'are,* the Old Man started, deadly serious. *You're gonna learn.*

*The only thing you learn from the dead is how to get kilt. I'll find another camp.* The Kid thought this was the Truth, as he had heard from others and made it out to be so himself, and with such a statement bolstering his resolve and what he figured to be his next actions, he took a step for his pack with a mind to leave.

The Old Man had him fast—faster this time—and as once again he found himself dragged, the Kid had then not only the reminder of how bad he was at figuring, but the understanding that some truths ain't Truths at all, and he should probably be more discerning about the ones he bet hisself on, because on the scale of lessons learned mistaking one for the other, this might actually be lesser than the rest. Which was no help whatsoever as those rough hands, stronger than any of them machines that lay twisted and ruined outside, shoved him close, closer now, right up to the face of one'a them workers.

Quiet, with no wane or wax. Potentially the only true serenity, for everything else was conflict to a greater or lesser degree. A conflict as the Kid was in, trying to move against the unyielding grip of the Old Man, who finally spoke. *When you sleep, they will speak to you. They will tell you stories. They will tell you the Truth.* Satisfied, both with what he'd said and with the fact the Kid had heard him, he let the Kid go. The Kid took the opportunity to pull back and look away, where he saw the Old Man smoothing out another cot, just nearby, before he continued. *And you'll gaze into that abyss, wonderin' if there ain't something there but hurt, despair, sorrow, damnation, hatred. And you'll keep going, and you'll think to yourself, maybe I just push on. Maybe it gets better. Maybe there's more, deeper down. And you'll keep looking, 'cause y'were always taught there can't be all that bad, with no good there to balance it out. Ye read them Old Books, heard all them tales, what with folks reassuring themselves there can't be a life that's all suffering; there has to be a reprieve at the end. At the very least, it's owed to us: there has to be a reprieve at the end.* The Old Man knelt. He was stiff, now, and it hurt. But the hurt didn't matter. He never looked away as he finished. *It's a damnable lie. There's no reward. No light. No nothin' after this 'cept ... nothin'.*

*If that's true,* the Kid said, *then why bother? Why do anything but kill, and whore, and drink, if ye're just gonna end up like these men here? Or like Him, out there? What's the point?*

*Well now. That's the question, ain't it?* Maybe even a question the Old Man himself didn't quite have the answer for, even as he asked it. *That's the part that's up to you.*

And like he was wont to do, as the Kid was starting to understand and almost anticipate, the Old Man then bowed his head in silence. This time, though, the Kid noticed something'd changed, the way you only noticed certain things when there was another like thing nearby to let you know how close they was. This silence in the Old Man, with his head bowed that way, was no different than the silence of the dead. A comparison drove home as the Kid felt his eyes drawn to the side there, where he hadn't looked properly before. A dead man stared back. No mushrooms, these were still eyes, and they locked on the Kid's; even though there was nothing behind them but silence, they still held him. Gone, but still watching. And though he knew there was nothing there, that it didn't make any difference where he was, he moved a bit farther away, to a different cot.

*They ain't gonna come back here tonight, you think? Burn the rest of this place?* Different words, but the same question he'd asked before, and like before, he knew enough the answer once he'd put his mind to it a little. *Course not. We're safe here.* The Kid lay down, and the stiffness of the cot matched the rigid form his body took, as his muscles stayed tight. He pulled his rifle close, both sets of knuckles white, instead'a leaving it close by where it normally should'a been. Close as he held it, it didn't feel close enough, though the Kid couldn't be sure of the difference exactly. Even with the rifle, those muscles wouldn't relax. He could blame it on the cot, though if he were being honest he knew any given night before this one he could'a slept more or less fine on the thing. He closed his eyes, having heard once that one would lead to the other if you just kept it up long enough, and he suddenly realized to himself that he didn't remember any of the prayers he was taught, and that this would'a been the perfect time to have remembered one of them.

And it was later, much later, when what passed for a door in what used to be a barracks opened, letting in a little of what little light there was outside. What little light there was was just enough to create a silhouette, to illuminate enough of a figure of a man, for the Kid to know that the figure entered the room and then shut the door, casting what used to be a barracks again into darkness.

The Kid was awake. Whether he had been the entire time or if this was a new development was immaterial; what mattered is he was awake, and petrified as he was, the Kid knew there was someone in what used to be the barracks with them.

*You awake?* he tried to whisper, hoping he could find that balance of the right one hearing him and the wrong one not. There was no response, until the footsteps started, and terror came with each one, telling the awful story of what was gonna happen to the Kid once they got there; each heel hitting that hard ground, sharp and deliberate, came with it a tale of what the outcome would be.

*Someone's here,* the Kid choked out, more forceful this time. Still not as loud as the footsteps, but damnit it should'a been loud enough to be heard.

The Kid still couldn't bring himself to move as the steps got closer. He heard a shuffle and a snap, and he wasn't sure how he'd known it, but that to him was the sound of the footsteps going out of their way to kick one of the crosses over, never mindin' what it was supposed to do or represent, before they came again on their way toward him. Then the fear backed down a minute and let room in his mind so's the Kid could remember: his rifle.

It weren't where it had been—in his hands—nor where it should have been, close by enough that he'd'a reached for it without much trouble, no. It simply wasn't there. Unfortunately—or maybe not, for sometimes these things were best if they was done and over with quick—the Kid didn't have time to wonder where it had gone, because it was then the footsteps stopped, and up above him, looking down, stood the Old Man.

Darkness swirled all around him, something darker than everything else in what was left of the barracks, but there was no mistaking it was him. The Old Man looked over to where the Kid's hands had fished and felt about, just off to the side there, then looked back up to the Kid and said to him, *Was you plannin' to kill me?*

The Kid couldn't respond; there was no right response to a question like that. He couldn't move, neither. He just stared up, up at the darkness swirling about him, leaning down closer now.

*Could ye do it, if ye had to? If it was just you and me?* The Old Man was leaning down close enough now to reach out with those rough hands, place them iron grips around the Kid's throat. In an instant, the darkness poured over the Kid like a rain falling. It poured in sheets and torrents from the Old Man, as he squeezed the light outta the Kid. *Or would you be afeared, like this?* And he was right, of course, for the darkness pouring down over the Kid might have carried terror with it as well. And the Kid struggled, but the fear, and darkness, and that iron grip, simply wouldn't let go.

*Ain't like you thought, is it?* The Kid had known what the Old Man was doing. Trying to teach him lessons. Trying to make him understand the Truth about what the Kid had set out to do, so's maybe the Kid wouldn't be so keen to do it. But afeared or not the Kid still had the fire in his eyes, and he still knew what he had set his mind to, and no man was gonna stop him in it. It was then, in that fleeting moment where the Kid knew he was gonna fight right up 'til the end, that those eyes'a fire caught a flicker of light through the rain of darkness, and he realized it was the light streaming through from outside what might have once been a barracks, reflecting off the hammer of the Old Man's holstered gun.

*Never is,* the Old Man kept on, and it was clear he hadn't seen what the Kid had, didn't know what the Kid knew.

*Never what you expect.* He was still talkin', even as the Kid shifted his weight, his arms half-limp before they could slip free one of the revolvers from its holster. And what strength he had was fading as he told his hands and arms to move in such a way as to turn that gun round, so's the barrel was pointed where he wanted it to go, and it might'a been the last thing that finger ever did as that last bit'a light fell from his eyes right before he forced that trigger back and the hammer fell like the darkness had before it.... .

THE KID STARTLED HIMSELF AWAKE, his hands tight around his rifle, right where he'd brought it to the night before. Everything was as it should be: the same bodies in the same cots, the light of morning shining through a thousand holes in the walls and ceiling of what used to be a barracks. Nearby, the Old Man sat on the edge of his own bed, using a straight razor to keep the ends of his beard neat. The Kid wasn't sure what he wanted to ask more: how—for he knew why—he did this without a mirror, and then also where he might'a gotten the razor. But the Kid put his mind to it a second and realized the first wasn't gonna get answered, and the second, well, he just as well preferred it didn't get answered neither.

*Whatever you saw, it was just a dream,* the Old Man told him. The Kid knew he was right, of course, but still needed a moment to convince himself of the fact. When the Old Man had finished with his beard, he folded up that razor and left it tidy on the edge of the bed, like it was gonna be waitin' there for whoever decided they was gonna use it next. *Sort your particulars out, and let's get on. We know they been here, so it ain't gonna take much to suss out which way they went.*

The Kid should have been excited by the thought, considering how it felt like his whole sense of purpose, his whole life, was given focus and meaning by those words. But in the time since, as they'd been walking, his thoughts were jumbled and his wants and desires and worries all clanged and clashed together. No matter how he tried, no matter what lessons he remembered, he couldn't get the thoughts to calm down and sort themselves out orderly like. And the noise of that clanging and clashing stayed with him for so long after a while it turned to constant fact and he stopped even hearing it.

## 7. *The Landscape, as Overrun by Nature*

IT WAS AN UNFAIR AND misleading thing to call Mother Nature by a single name, as though it was a cohesive unit what moved with a purpose. Nature was a thousand things, all acting on their own, none with any regard to th'other, and whatever

came of all those forces acting on any one thing didn't concern
any of the individuals, for they'd already had their own way and
didn't mind much of anything else. So as the Kid and the Old
Man walked down what may have one time or another been a
road, everything that stood and sprouted around them was hard
to differentiate, since nature had long since been having its way
in the haphazard fashion it always did.

The Kid's eyes were open, sharp, checking for movement
amongst what used to be manufactured things and were now
natural features. They weren't moving fast, so's now he could
have his rifle at the ready, just in case he spotted something he
was looking for. He figured if he'd had time, if he didn't have a
need to keep his eyes focused and fixed for movement, he could
have likely sussed what things out there once were. But for now
there was no time, so he put such concerns out of his mind, and
focused on other things what didn't require keen eyes to spot,
but maybe just a mind and ears instead.

*How'd you know my mother?* he asked the Old Man. By this time,
it was the comfortable type'a speaking one did with a casual
friend, someone you'd spent enough time with that you could
skip some of the formalities and just chat.

Before the Old Man could answer, the Kid saw a flash of
memory dart past him, and a slight smile cinch his face. *We
traveled together. Long time ago,* the Old Man said, and there was
another something not quite a smile, and them scars got tight
a second, before he sent that memory to a different place than
the first, and continued on with his answer. Casual, too, like the
Kid's question. *Long time ago. Back when we was all tryin' to do
some good.*

*What was she like?* the Kid kept on, the same kind'a casual.

*Well now. Shouldn't you have your own ideas a'that?* It was a fair point, and the Old Man meant it. Not in the way he meant some'a the lessons he'd said to the Kid before, more in the way that the Old Man knew how these things went—it'd happened to him a thousand times over—and he didn't wanna take away from the Kid's own memories, for he knew memories were a fragile thing. They could often be run roughshod over by new thoughts and speeches and ideas from other folks, until your own memories, what you held to be the Truth of a person, were at least mixed and muddled, if not torn up and thrown out entirely.

Even if the Kid didn't know all that, didn't know the pitfalls and traps to avoid with a question of that kind, he'd had an entirely different reason to ask. *I only remember her bein' old,* the Kid said. *She would never talk about the times before, and nothin' about her self, much.* He likely would'a kept going, but there was one of those flits of movement—only just more real than a memory—out the corner of his eye, and as fast as he had that rifle up to his cheek and his eyes down the sights, that movement was just a bit faster, and he'd just missed it.

The Kid couldn't hide the disappointment in what he saw as another in a string of failures, and there was a muttering and a hitch in his step as he had to bring himself back up to normal again. The Old Man noticed all this without looking—maybe 'cause he'd seen it happen before or maybe he just knew that was the way of people—and didn't break stride. *Told you, I'll find us something,* the Old Man reassured him, and he meant it, too. Whether the Kid believed him or not was kinda aside the point, since he was intending to keep a look out anyway, figuring him searching his way and the Old Man his was just gonna add up to more chance of one of them finding what they was looking for.

*She told me about you, though. Just a little,* the Kid said, and hearing those words and what it was they must'a meant gave the Old Man a slight hitch in his walk, as he had to take a couple different memories that came a'calling and put them back in the places they belonged before he could answer in a befitting way.

*Well, most of that ain't something a kid should hear.* And the Old Man meant that too.

*Hey now,* the Kid started, in that casual way he now felt comfortable using, even when standin' up for himself. *You need to stop callin' me that. I ain't a kid. I'm … Well, I don't know how old I am exactly, but I know I'm not a kid.*

A statement like that, with a man defending hisself and opening up and letting you in to see a little of what makes him vulnerable … Well, it's easy for another man of a certain kind of mind to find a response what speaks to laughter, joshing the other man, poking at where he's just shown a hole. But the Old Man was long past all such nonsense, and what's more the Kid had made a valid point of his own, and spoke comfortable, too, so the Old Man felt it was only fair he respond in the ways in which he was responded to himself.

The Old Man gave the Kid a once-over. Looked at him properly, for what the Kid felt like was the first time. It wasn't like when they'd first met—and damn it all if he could remember how long ago that'd been now—when the Old Man had grabbed his face with those rough hands and studied him like he did. No, for the first time now the Kid felt like the Old Man was looking at him, and really saw him. Not just eyes of fire and fear, not just a scared hand reaching for a rifle, but a whole creature, understanding him as more than just the sum of parts and pieces and motivations and words and thoughts. Bein' seen like that, it was what so many men think they want, and in fact ask for …

but often that's just a way of deflecting others from looking at the parts of 'em they don't like and don't feel like changing. That kinda look makes a man uncomfortable more often than not, but this time it didn't. The Kid didn't feel a need to hide that or lie or puff himself up or anything else. He wasn't sure why, and for all his time after these things happened, he couldn't'a broken it down and explained it; this just wasn't one of those kind of studying looks that made a man uncomfortable is all.

A once-over like that feels like it takes a lifetime; fact is, it's called a once-over because it just takes the once, which ain't long at all. *Prob'ly not much more than thirty, way we used to tell the passing of the years.* The Old Man was matter-of-fact, so much so the Kid wouldn't have said different even if he knew otherwise. *But ain't just how long you been here, kid. It's the things you see. Those are what change you and make ye grow. It's those moments, not the years, that decide when you ain't a kid no more.*

Those were the kind of words that could cut a man to his core, if he were inclined to believe 'em. The Kid knew what the Old Man said had merit, he just felt like it didn't apply to him was all. *I've seen plenty,* the Kid said back, and he meant it, too.

*Y'seen nothing.* The Old Man was dismissive, back to the way he spoke everything in riddles masquerading as lessons—leastways that's how it felt to the Kid. *And you should be thankful for it. Back there, what you thought looked like you? You'll argue with me on it, but I tell you this: it's good you don't know any better. It's good you can't see what it really looks like. What it really is.*

*And what do you see?* The Kid didn't mean that as a challenge; it was another one of those genuine questions he really did think he wanted the answer to. Course, whether he did or not the Old Man didn't answer, and the Kid knew he wasn't gonna the second the question left his mouth. He kept up with the Old

Man, just walking for a while, before he said, *She told me where them scars come from.*

And that stopped the Old Man. There were too many memories—or maybe just the one, big, painful one—that stopped him dead step, so's he even needed to think a moment and force his foot back to the ground there. *Did she now?* The Old Man sniffed the air after he spoke, and then the Kid started thinking maybe he hadn't stopped because of the question after all.

*She told me 'bout what you did. How you saved all them people.* The Kid didn't have a memory of his own to go along with the words, but it was clear from how he spoke that he'd once heard enough to have what felt like a memory about 'em as well.

*Thought you said she didn't tell you much about me?* The Old Man tossed the words as an aside and was following his nose now, which gave further credence to the idea that the Kid's words weren't what stopped him in the first place, and he felt like a damn fool for even thinkin' that.

*She told me enough.* The Kid followed him without really thinking. Curiosity forced his feet, wanting to know just what must'a touched the Old Man's nose.

The Old Man continued along, following the scent he'd caught, and came to a tree. For a moment there he looked almost as confused as the Kid did; then, like he was puttin' a puzzle together, the Old Man ran those rough hands down the length of rougher bark—likely the only thing round here older than he was, if the Kid felt like joshing the man—and felt along the ground, looking for something with those hands.

*If she did that, you wouldn't'a never come lookin for me.* The Old Man stopped talking, whether he had anything left to say, then scraped and scrabbled with those rough old hands, what was left of nails pulling that loamy dirt aside like he was born to it, until he found something. With a bit of work, the Old Man pulled free a small, gnarled root, 'bout the size of a palm's width, though twisted and looped around on itself so's to indicate if it was stretched out it could'a been a sight longer. It was only as thin around as a finger. When the Old Man pulled free a couple more and offered one up to the Kid, the Kid took a sniff, just to see what all the Old Man's fuss was about, and what touched his nose from that made him recoil and cough, owing as to the smell being worse than the sight. The Old Man smiled and thoughtfully packed the dirt back round into the hole, making sure not to pack it down too tight so others could grow in its place, and the Kid looked at him for a second like he'd gone mad, being happy to find something like—

—A blur, barely a streak, of movement just past the corner of his eye, and almost all at once the rifle touched the cheek and the eyes touched those iron sights at the end of the barrel and the finger touched the trigger.

OVER A SMALL FIRE, ROOTS and rabbit cooked on opposite sides. The rabbit was a scrawny, grizzled old thing, only a bit larger than the roots, and depending which way each was turned on the end of their little stick sometimes it was hard to tell which was which. The Old Man didn't cook the roots long—there weren't much point to it—and each bite he took the Kid grimaced, like he could see just how tough and sour them things were.

*I know what yer thinking,* the Old Man said between bites, and he smiled as he talked casual, the way two men comfortable with each other on the road should. *And yer right. There ain't a thing left in creation, not that I know of leastways, makes these old things palatable. But that don't matter much, given the circumstances.*

The Kid indicated the stick which indicated the rabbit, still turning this way and that, trying to help it from suffering the same culinary fate as the roots. *You're welcome to some of this, if ye like.* It was a genuine offer, but said with a little smirk in such a way as to let the Old Man knew he felt like he'd won, so's he was joshing a little.

*You go right ahead.* The Old Man was halfway between joshing and being serious himself.

*No, I mean it.* The Kid had to study the rabbit again, just to make sure, before he finished, *Plenty to go round.*

*Not always.* The Old Man tucked into another one of those roots, and laughed at the little game they was playing, joshing each other … but maybe there was a lesson to be learned in all of it as well. The time made the Kid think of the stories he'd heard about the way things was before, when folks who lived nearby would come round and visit, not for no reason, not to help with works that needed doing, but just to sit a spell and while away the time in fellowship. It was a hard thing for him to make hisself imagine, growing up as he did, always on the move, work to be done, traveling hither and yon without nothing much to show for it, never making friends, losing the friends he did make, not having time for much else besides. It was difficult to think on, to remember all those things, and often as it did happen he would remind himself to ignore it, not to dwell on the past, as he was taught, and to focus on what was happening in the present moment, even without concern for the what ifs of the future. There weren't no time for such things, moving about as he did when a child, and when there was, maybe later on down the road, he could worry about it then.

It was getting late as they kept walking, and more often the Kid's thoughts would turn to camp ... where to set up, and more importantly, when, when the Old Man gave him a tap to fix his mind, and pointed up a ways:

A bouncing, weaving dragon of lights—lanterns and torches— their amber eyes and flared halos cutting a swath through the darkness, a thousand individuals bleeding into one indistinguishable miasma. There was no mistaking a held light from a distance, not when the sun was low behind the trees, and there was no mistaking how many folks was holding 'em. The uniformity of the movement, the fact that each and every space held a light, meant that this could only be an army.

The Kid was awestruck, watching that serpent weave its way along what would be their same path, albeit farther ahead, now coming up to cresting the little hill that put them in sight in the first place, and the Kid imagined them oozing again down the far side, creating a hypnotic pattern in the distance.

The Old Man saw no beauty in the thing, found no fascination in the undulating beast of light and fire. This was not an artifact to be appreciated; to him, this was a tool to be used. Without ceremony or consideration, he pulled the Kid down, off the path, down, into a gulley, down, below the tree line.

Then the Old Man quickened their pace. Tired as he was before, the Kid was now alert and focused, and it wasn't long before he and the Old Man caught up alongside that dragon of carried lights. They kept out of sight even as they hurried, past the indistinguishable lines of men, each so similar to the next so as to be no different than stalks of wheat blowing in a steady breeze.

*How many of 'em you think are up there?* The Kid was still enthralled at the sight, and his breathless whisper could have been because he was half dumbstruck, or it could have been that he still had his wits about him and knew better than to speak loud in the presence of the dragon. But none of that wouldn't have mattered, since the distance and flutter of the trees combined with the bootsteps and crackle of fires and low muttering like men do to keep themselves busy while walking in an endless parade like this, and it all collected into a din that was at the same time loud enough to mask most any reasonable noise and quiet enough that any individual could'a just as easily forgot it was there.

*Too many,* the Old Man said, as he searched and studied their ranks, like he was sizing up which of the flock was gonna end up a meal … or, more likely knowing his way of doing things as the Kid had learned, which of the dozens of apples were gonna have to be the one to come down off'a the tree, knowing you only got one pick.

*You think He's there?* The Kid hadn't known that was gonna be the question 'til he asked it, when the fear and the what if of the thought suddenly hit him.

*No.* The Old Man replied with a certainty that almost took the Kid aback, but he didn't have time to follow up with just how in the hell he would so surely know that before the Old Man continued, *But one of 'em might'n point us in the right direction,* and then he moved quick, straight up the side of the embankment, closer to the army.

Too close, the Kid thought, as he followed, and dropped his voice down even quieter than it'd been before. *You outta your mind? They're gonna see you.*

*They're just men,* the Old Man said, and the Kid honestly weren't sure exactly why he thought that were an answer.

*Doesn't mean we should be walkin' up there right into the middle of 'em.*

*They're just men,* the Old Man said again, as he got even closer now. And the Kid followed him, though he was reluctant, and a sight more cautious. Of course, it wouldn't matter how cautious he was if the Old Man was up there tromping around making whatever noise he wanted, but the Kid just couldn't help himself but follow.

... *Evil men,* the Kid said, as he found a little ridgeway it seemed the Old Man had been walking along, and from there the two stalked the army. Funny, that: two after many, lambs after lions.

*Ain't no such thing.* As they talked, the Old Man never took his eyes off all those men, seeing the wheat through the breeze, like he was figuring which one to pick.

*There is if they're following Him.* The Kid thought that was the kind of thing what spoke for itself, and he said it with the kind of certainty he thought said it all.

*Just means they been led down a different path is all.* The Old Man indicated up in the direction of a random row of men that looked like every other row of men. *But there for grace goes either of us. Do well not to forget such things.*

*That ain't true,* the Kid said. That was another one he knew deep in his bones weren't right. *That kinda thing is either in you or it ain't. To stand up against your fellow man, bringing war? That's not in me.*

*You aim to bring war on Him, don'tcha?* The Old Man said it casual, the way he'd toss out a question about what a man had for dinner. But the Kid had to consider his response careful, and he took a moment to. He felt this was important, even if it was just for him to know.

*… He's evil.* The Kid could see their faces, now. They weren't all quite the same, but they was … similar. Trick of the light, maybe, or the way they was all marching in that hypnotic pattern of theirs, or the fact they was able to keep all neatly trimmed, and the hats they wore was just like so, and their jackets patched right. All the things that needed to look the same did, and it queered the sense of anything else that could be different.

The Old Man stopped, leaned himself against a tree, with his back to the army. He was still facing the Kid, who was still facing the army, but the Old Man closed his eyes, and he listened, calm and gentle, even as he talked the same way. *He's a part of humanity. And we all got Him inside us. Some just got more than others.*

The Old Man heard something then—a wax in the quiet. And well before the Kid could have been able to speak a response, even if he'd had one, the Old Man whistled. It was sharp, clean, clear. It was not like a bird's call—too distinct for that—and sounded through the woods just right, so's it caught the attention of a Soldier. He was one amongst many, but it was he who heard it, he who wondered what it was if'n not a bird, and he who fumbled half a step, and he, who in that fumble, dropped what he'd been carrying in his off hand.

**THE KID SAW THE LIGHTER land.** Its metal reflected the line of torches and lanterns in order, making sure it weren't never lost as long as the army kept marching by. The Kid was hypnotized by that reflection the same as he had been the line of men carrying the torches causing it, and though it was out of his reach, it most certainly weren't gonna be lost, the way it shone on the mossy ground of the forest there.

Good thing, too, as the Soldier stepped his way out of the line—even the way he fell out from the others felt regimental, like any of 'em would'a done it exactly the same—and he came through the trees and on down a little slip of the embankment. It was just a few steps, but it put him out of sight of the others, depending on if they was looking for him in just the right way, which none of 'em was doing, because none of the rest of 'em was.

The Soldier saw the light reflecting just the right way on that lighter, and he counted his luck that he'd come down just this way and looked in just that place, and he reached for that little thing that wouldn't'a meant much to anyone else, but meant a lot to him, and as chance would have it he reached down in just such a way that he ended up looking right at the Kid.

The army kept moving, causing that same din, trailing that same light over the whole of creation, but that was all that let either of them know the world was still turning, instead'a time having stopped then and there. The two stared at each other, an eternity in that moment. They was both young—still kids, in a way of looking at things—both scared, and both confused.

Both hands twitched, hovering near their weapons. Weren't one wearing a hat just like so, and th'other having had patched up his jacket a thousand times over, and one carried a rifle slung over his back and the other an old repeater at his waist, each could'a been mistaken for the other, after a fashion. There was no mistaking what was happening, though, as those two hands hoverin' over those two weapons said it straight—each was to kill the other. Neither wanted to do it, and both hoped they wouldn't have to. That much was clear in the hovering instead'a the pointing.

It was the Kid that broke first, not as a measure of weakness or fear, but as an understanding of what needed to happen to stop them hands doing what they didn't want to do. His eyes flicked down to the lighter, still reflecting the light, on the mossy ground there.

*Ain't that a funny thing,* the Kid said, soft and gentle with his voice, the same way he was when he held up his hand, away from and off the rifle, reaching instead for a shape in a pocket. *I got one just like it.* He slipped his own lighter out of that pocket, and held it up so it too caught the light from the torches and lanterns, and the Soldier could tear his eyes off the Kid and up to that other lighter—even though maybe it could'a been a trick—because, well, when someone showed you a thing what else was a man to do. *Damn thing's all but empty, though.* The Kid held it next to his ear and shook it, as though to prove a point, as though the sounds could'a touched the Soldier's ear as well.

Whether they might have or not, the Soldier stayed tense, still not sure what to make of all that had happened in so short a time, and without having any idea what else to do he just sorta said the first thing that come to his head, which was always the way he was doing things, though folks often told him it weren't necessarily the best idea and maybe he should stop it, all things considered.

*My paw gimme this'n, 'fores I strucked out on my own,* the Soldier said, in his peculiar way of talking that let the Kid know he was having some trouble with it. There was no mistaking that type of peculiar; the Kid had heard stories of folks with such ways, their troubles and whatnot, and though he hadn't met one that he knew of as 'til now, there was no mistaking such a thing.

With less trouble than he'd had talking, the Soldier reached down and picked up his own lighter. He'd always been good at such things—reachin' and liftin' and whatnot—and was a solid hand about town and felt pride in when he could help doing things others might not. It had been what led him here, to this army, when a man told him a soldier could do the things he was good at in service of something even bigger than helping out the folks around town. And the Soldier, well, helping people sounded good, and he liked doing what he was good at, and so he went along. He didn't have to speak much, which suited him fine; he was good at listening, and he could keep walking all day if'n he had to, and as long as the directions weren't too complicated he could do most things he was told.

The Soldier's mind had wandered to all those places and weren't yet on its way back when he heard the Kid speak to him. *This was a birthday gift, from my mother.*

The Soldier looked up again to the Kid's lighter, and he studied it with his eyes even as he studied his own with his gentle hands. And the Kid wasn't sure if maybe it was a trick of the light reflecting as it was, but maybe there had been a wetness in the corner of that Soldier's eyes, as he brought up memories that were a bit harder for him to reach for, though he cherished them nonetheless for it.

*If'n you want, mebbe we could trade'm?* The Soldier had looked back to the Kid by now. His memories—and whatever trick of the light was there—had gone, replaced by a love and understanding and sympathy that the Kid had never seen before. The Soldier held his own lighter up to his ear, just like the Kid had done, and shook it, just like the Kid had done, in case the sounds could touch the Kid's ears as the Kid had thought maybe his had done the same but opposite. *This'n's 'bout full already, and it ain't much fer me to refull yours when we stop?*

The Kid wasn't sure why, but he was apprehensive. *That's generous of you to offer,* he started, and realized maybe that was why … because he hadn't seen much of anything resembling generosity of any kind, and certainly not offers, that didn't come with an anchor of obligation in return that a man had to drag around with him a long ways were he to take it up.

*Y'do same fer me, I bet, inna diff'rent time*, the Soldier said, and this came with no anchor, nothing to weight the trade. Nothing but a man offering another something he needed, not on account'a getting something back, but on account'a the other man needing something the first had to give. It was so honest that the Kid didn't even flinch as the Soldier took a step forward and pushed his hand out, the lighter once held tight now sitting loose on his palm, quivering just a little.

*I know that'n must be special to ye, come from yer mammy like it did. But mebbe they can keep bein' special to the each of us, only in another way?* The Soldier's eyes were honest, sincere. This was pure. This was Truth.

There was no tension left when the Kid made the trade. Their two hands met a moment, an unsaid thank you passing in the touch. After was an awkward silence, since everything until then was predicated on the tension and the worries, and now without it, neither man was sure what was supposed to fill the space, until the Kid nodded up at the rest of the army, still passing just mostly out of sight through the trees.

*Where you folks headed?* the Kid asked, in that comfortable way one would speak to a friend.

*Dunno. Jus' marchin' long the river. They'd already found what they'n's lookin fer previous, so we're movin on, I guess.*

*... What'd they find?* The Kid was trying not to seem overly interested, which matched him not really wanting to know the answer.

*Never asked*, the Soldier said, before he realized, *Ought'a be gettin back.* He had smiled and gave a little wave like one does when they're not sure what else to do in that moment, and the Kid barely had time to smile back before the Soldier was up the embankment and back into a place in the line—not his place, for that was long since gone, but any other was just the same, really—and had disappeared.

The Kid was left staring as the army passed, every one row the same as the one before ... all but one, he thought now. The Old Man went back down the embankment, back down to where they was walking before. Though just before he did, before the trees and distance would mean the Kid wouldn't hear what he said, he tossed a few words back up for the Kid to hear over the din of it all.

*... No sir. No such thing as evil.*

## 8. A River, Barely Moving

IT WAS A WIDE, DAUNTING thing. From a distance, the Kid had thought it looked like they might simply cross it on foot, thick and slow-going as it was. But up close it was different, as so many things are. The Kid grew up near one, and in small towns like his, the river—not this river, but any river—was a part of their lives. They had to know its moods and swells and eddies better than they knew their own, since the river's moods could destroy much quicker—and much more—than a man's could.

The Kid stood along the bank and tossed a few rocks its way, respectful, like an offering. When he was younger, he'd done this just as a way to pass the time. But as he grew, he learned how to see the way the ripples moved and the sound carried, and suss what mood the river was in, and whether it was safe to do whatever he had planned. The Kid had also sat and heard stories of how the river—not this river, but any river—were like time itself: always moving at its own pace, not to stop for no man, to be appreciated and understood and used as well as one can, but never to be changed, controlled, or stopped. The Kid enjoyed thinking of it in that way, and always got a kick out of the idea that he was tossing little stones into time itself.

Surely enough, time hadn't stopped, as the Kid realized the Old Man was still walking, and if he wanted to ask the question that'd just popped into his head, he best catch up.

*Was it always like this? Was He always this powerful?* the Kid asked, and it wasn't until much later, when he'd replayed this moment in his mind a thousand times over, did he realize there was some kind of poetry in asking such a question next to the river. This river.

*No. But it's been heading this way from the beginning.* The way the Old Man spoke, it was like he was looking ahead, but to something that had already happened. *Entropy's on His side.*

*How's that?* the Kid wanted to know.

*Any time a man acts with rage, or lust, or avarice … it takes 'em a bit closer to Him. Strive all ye want, no one's perfect. Everyone falls eventually. A man is limited. He recognizes his own mortality, gets impatient, envious, frustrated. Him? He just waits. Has all the time in the world.* The Old Man tossed a stone of his own into the river—the Kid hadn't even seen him pick one up—and it caught on the surface for a second, buoyed by a swell that the Kid didn't like the look of, before it sank. *When it got bad the first time,* the Old Man continued, *that was soon before you were born. It was much like this; He rose up, brought His armies forth, laid waste to the land.* The Old Man needed a breath before he could speak the rest. *Left us with what ye see now.*

The Kid thought for a moment. It was hard to comprehend, being something that he had no comparison for; what was "before" versus "is"? How could he even begin to understand the way something used to be, when he himself had never experienced it? It was left to the imagination, which was a pale replacement for experience. So instead of being lost in moments and considerations he could never understand, the Kid focused on the events he could, and asked, *And that's when you fought Him?*

The Old Man took some time to answer. *Yeah. But I was scared.* He looked farther up the river now, *I saw what was waiting for me, and turned away before it was finished.* He looked back the other way now, damning himself, fighting back against a memory, the scars cinching in his face. *A piece of Him was left. All He had to do was bide His time.*

Amidst all this, the Kid absently tossed a stone into the river. He was surprised to see this time it didn't leave no ripples.

*That's why I came at first to stop ye,* the Old Man continued, and the Kid wasn't sure if he'd seen the stone or not. *I been down this path. I took every step you're taking now. And I was scared for ye, on account of my own failures.*

*Tell me what went wrong, then,* the Kid said, excited. This was the kind of learning he was hoping to get from the Old Man in the first place, something that might help in his own quest, give him an understanding of what he was up against and what he could do different. *What happened?*

*Ye can't fight fire with fire.*

The Kid got struck dumb by that; it wasn't the kind of learning he was hoping for, after all. *You talk just like the men in them Old Books*, he said, disappointed.

*Funny how that happens*, the Old Man said through half a chuckle.

But any focus the Kid might have had on the Old Man's words, and that little twist that accompanied them, was lost as they rounded a bend. Across the river, at a narrow point, just off in a little channel, was a skiff, flat and open. Most of the wood had rotted long beyond use, that much was clear even at this distance. It was barely tied to its little dock—that poor thing not in much better shape—since frankly, it didn't seem like it was gonna go anywhere even if it weren't. The Kid was less interested in the seaworthiness of the skiff and more interested in the woman that manned the thing. She was old and withered, leaned far over on a cane, though her footing was sound and steadfast regardless. The river pushed a little harder over there it seemed, as the skiff rocked back and forth some, but she didn't seem to notice. Simply kept her eyes on the Old Man, followed him with her eyes as they walked, until both was out of sight again.

The Old Man had watched her, too, the whole time. He still watched her, in fact, even after she was out of sight, and he said to the Kid, *You sure you wanna keep on, kid?*

The Kid almost didn't understand the question. *We come this far, ain't we?* Of course he wanted to keep going. And the Old Man watched her a moment longer, even though of course he couldn't see her anymore, the way the Kid thought it. And they kept going because they were already going. Like the river, like time itself, what other choice did they have?

## 9. *There was a House on a Hill*

IT WAS AN OPULENT THING. Starting from its gate, made for looks as much as anything, though it was clear it once did its job as proper as a gate could be expected to. It stood before a long driveway, which curled and twisted for no reason at all, but for maybe to make someone wait just a little longer to get up there, and possibly rethink what he was planning to be there for in the first place. Hard to know why people made choices like those, but none of them mattered now, for there weren't choices like that left. Now, there was barbed wire laid everywhere: wrapped around that gate, weaving through that twisted driveway, scattered and layered thick, everywhere in between.

There was makeshift buildings, constructed different than everything else, posted up on either side of the gate, with more of them farther up along that drive, nearer to where the house sat up in the fog. Where they'd been put led the Kid to believe they were likely made to be guard towers; he could only guess what they might have been guarding against, given all the things a man like this might want to keep out.

Regardless what their intention was, the towers hadn't worked. The gate was bent and twisted in places, tucked in on itself in a way that made it easier to get over. It had been repaired—twisted back to which way it was supposed to be—then attacked and bent again. If ye knew a little about metalwork—the Kid had seen one or two things made over a forge—it was easy enough to tell when things weren't the way they were supposed to be. And in some spots on this gate, that was putting it lightly.

*The hell happened here?* the Kid wondered aloud, as much to himself as the Old Man. He went over to examine everything

more closely, and almost missed the reply the Old Man muttered
under his breath,

*Somethin' like that.*

The Kid ran his hands across some of the bottom rails of the
metal, where it'd sunk into the ground. There were deep gouges,
cut right into the steel, like it'd been torn and pulled at, and little
bits of it had come away. There were marks and scratches like
that all over; it was terrifying to think of all the ways it could
have ended up like this, and all the things that could'a caused
it … and the Kid had to stop. He had to focus on something
different, something present, something he could do.

*Think someone's still in there?* he asked, as he looked up through
that sea of twisted and craven wire, toward the house way up on
the hill, situated in the fog.

*'M sure of it,* the Old Man said, barely looking at the place.
Looking anywhere but there.

The Kid took the response as tacit approval of what he'd already
decided his plan was. He felt like at this point he knew the Old
Man well enough that he'd more than likely guess what the Kid
was thinking, and if'n he didn't approve—tacitly or otherwise—
he would make his case known, and they could have one of their
next dozen arguments of the day. So when the Kid reached for
the gate, he was surprised when the Old Man's hand shot out
like a snake and grabbed his.

*Don't wanna do that,* the Old Man said, as he moved the Kid's
hand away from where he was going to open the gate, to a bent
and twisted part of the fencing that, on second glance, the Kid
saw was shaped to resemble something like a cross. It was one
of those things you'd never see at first glance, but once you had,

you couldn't unsee it. As such, even as they spoke, the Kid kept finding his eyes drawn to the thing, staring at it, studying it.

*There for a reason,* the Old Man said. He didn't have to look at the cross anymore. He'd seen enough, no doubt.

*Aren't they just trying to keep those things out?* the Kid asked, still looking at the cross, then to the gouges on the metal, then back up to the cross. He knew they were all connected—everything was connected—but he'd be damned if he knew how.

*Maybe.*

*Well, what if they need help?* The Kid pulled his hand away—the Old Man let him—and reached for the gate again. He fought against time and rust and everything else that had put it all in the wrong place, and finally when he set his feet and put his body into it he managed to jerk the gate open. The Kid eyed the path first, searching for the best way through all that wire from a theoretic standpoint before he tried the actual traverse of the damned stuff, then started up the driveway.

*You comin'?* he asked the Old Man. It was meant to be rhetorical, seeing as how he thought he knew the way the Old Man did things by now.

*I'll be along,* the Old Man responded, and that most certainly wasn't what the Kid was expecting to hear, not that he understood what and when exactly the Old Man meant by it, neither. So he just decided to ignore what meanings lay below the surface, and in this moment just do what he thought was right.

**INSIDE THE HOUSE WERE OSTENTATIOUS and unnecessary signs of wealth.** Unnecessary was a term usually decided in the mind of the beholder, but in this case the Kid felt comfortable that he would'a spoken for most people these days. What was here had all been ransacked and overturned and then tidied up in a way and overturned and ransacked again. The door had creaked open almost of its own accord when the Kid came in. It creaked closed most certainly of its own accord once he was inside proper.

*Hello?* the Kid called out, partially remembering his manners, that he was to announce himself in a case where people might not know he was there, and also because he was looking to find out if there was in fact people there who might not know about him.

He didn't hear anything so far, 'cept for the groans of the floor after each step he took on the old boards. These weren't rotted like so much of the other wood he'd come across recently, they weren't liable to break at any moment or with any step. These were fine boards made of fine wood, laid some time ago with a mind to stay where they was put, by a craftsman who knew their trade, not a random journeyman who could do a passable job at a fraction of the cost, which was all anyone could afford these days.

*I'm a friend,* he called out again. There was no concern with keeping quiet, mostly because there was no chance anybody nearby hadn't heard him the first time, and certainly if they was paying attention they knew where he was with every step he took. He still was careful, though, cautious, and as he made his way through the house he tried to keep his mind quiet, so's to take note of anything out of the ordinary. Unfortunate, then, that it was human nature to so often miss the things most obvious when you were most looking for them, as he walked right past a small mirror, hung on the wall, carefully covered up with glued-down paper and a small linen cloth.

The Kid was being as quiet as possible, listening through the still air. Behind him, all the way across the large room, was a door, just barely open, with a pair of eyes watching him through the crack. They were small, like a child's, and low to the ground, as a child's would be. But they didn't make any noise as they looked, and so the Kid couldn't tell they was there. The same way he didn't see along the upstairs balcony, with its beautifully worked balustrade, made of something fine like alabaster or ivory or another of those materials that a man like him never got a chance to see up close often enough to know it at a glance. It was from there, behind that gorgeous filigree and hand-carved designs, that a little girl watched him—she had the same eyes as the figure behind the crack in the door, about the same level above the ground, and she was as quiet as they was, so the Kid didn't know she was there neither.

It wasn't until a baby cried—a quick yelp, like the noise was cut off right after it happened, but just enough had escaped and gotten a chance to reach the Kid's ears—that the Kid noticed. Not that he noticed the eyes or the little girl, since they were both gone in the instant between that cry starting and stopping; no, it was only now that the Kid noticed anything. He froze, replaying that noise in his mind over and over, hoping to hear it again enough times to know where it came from and what it might'a meant. He knew right away he weren't gonna hear that cry again, but gave it long enough in silence just in case.

*Was just passing by. I can help.* Since he'd already given up his own silence, he didn't think there was much harm in calling out, but even then there was a caution and an unsure crack in his voice, which embarrassed him to no end, since he felt like if a man was coming to help others he couldn't be the one who was scared.

Ahead of him, there was another door. When he looked at it, the Kid realized a couple things: one, he wasn't sure if there'd been a door there before, which he should have known since he had been headin' in that general direction, whether he was trying to be quiet or not; two, and maybe more important, he didn't know if the door he wasn't sure had been there in the first place had already been open or not. Either way, the door was there, and it was open; just a crack, enough for him to see in if'n he was at the right angle, and definitely enough for whoever was in there to see out. And this wasn't a question—whether the door had been there and whether it had previously been open—those were all up for debate, but the Kid was certain there was someone inside, since he could see those eyes staring back at him.

They were barely visible, in the dark like everything was. But these eyes glowed, just a little—maybe they were catching some faraway light, like that dropped lighter had, whenever that had happened—only there was no faraway light here he could blame it on.

*He's been here,* the Father said. The Kid only figuring it was a father because the eyes were up high enough, and it was one'a them deep and authoritative voices that just sounded like a father, especially considering the Kid had just heard what sounded like a baby crying … and when you sorta put all those things together by the time you hear those couple words, it's accurate enough an idea for the moment.

*Who?* the Kid asked, as he took a step closer. He wasn't drawn toward the eyes or the door, it wasn't like that. He moved closer to give whoever was in there—whoever owned that terrified voice, that terrified set of eyes—the feeling that the Kid were in charge, that he could help.

*Him*, the Father said, incensed, like he was repeating himself.

*That's not possible*, the Kid responded. When he said that he looked out to the window, like he was gonna judge the distance and make up his mind to be certain, but he realized then the glass was boarded up, leaving him with no way to get his bearings, not that it would have mattered. He knew it couldn't have been true, whether he could see outside with his own eyes or not. He'd been there. He'd been traveling this whole time… . *He couldn't have made it this far yet.* More to the point, the Kid thought, he wouldn't have missed Him.

*You came from the river, issit?* The Father's voice had less authority, now. Had this been the first thing the Father said, the Kid never would'a thought of him as such. He would have been just another man. *You think you're heading out to meet Him?* It was like the Father was in pain as he squeezed out the rest of his words. *You're following where He's already been.* It was emphatic, like he was yelling, though his voice never rose.

The Kid needed a moment to consider this monumental accusation. If it were true, it made a mockery out of all he'd been through so far. It was probably for that reason, struck dumb as he was, that he didn't notice those children moving closer. The Father most certainly did, however—the glow in his eyes shifted just enough—and his next words were in a breathy panic, perfectly designed to grab the Kid's attention, just in case he were thinking of taking a look around.

*Give us a drink, will ya?* the Father asked, as he thrust a thin, clawing hand out through the doorway toward the Kid. The eyes—the rest of him—never got any closer, though it seemed he was straining and forcing the rest of himself against the doorway, like it was jammed somehow, and wouldn't open up past where it was. The Kid was taken aback by the forcefulness of the movement, the desperation suddenly visible in the glow. It was enough to focus his attention so's he would never have noticed those children getting closer, even if they had made a lick of noise as they moved across those same boards.

*Please ... so thirsty,* the Father said, again annoyed, but more angry now, like he was repeating something that he shouldn't have had to say in the first place. And the Kid, to his credit, always wanting to help people as he did, took his flask and was slow to offer it out, thinking to himself what harm could come, since worst of all things he could just get another flask one way or another.

When that hand grabbed hold of him, it was almost like the Kid was away from his own body, seeing everything happening to him from just above and behind, experiencing things from both inside and outside at once. He marveled at how strong that thin hand was—more like a lady's than a man's, and thin even for that—as it gripped him with a force different than the one the Old Man had brought to bear, though no less possible to pull away from. Associated with that was how easy it seemed the Father pulled him through that doorway, belying the strength in those wispy limbs. The Kid was mad at himself for not realizing there was nothing blocking that doorway, since it opened easy enough as soon as the ruse was over, and those damnable children were all inside it at once as well and the Kid was mad at himself for not noticing that no matter how much noise they did or didn't make, but all those thoughts stopped short and there weren't even time to yell out or reach back or hold on or nothing else along them lines before he was inside and the door was shut and all was quiet again.

**OUTSIDE, AT THE GATE,** THE Old Man watched. There wasn't a sound could be heard from down here, not a flash that came through them windows, boarded up as they were, but it didn't matter. He knew. He reached out to that bent and twisted part of the fencing, he grabbed his hand round that metal shaped to resemble a cross, and it didn't take more than a sharp tug for him to rend that metal like it was nothing at all. The Old Man tossed that cross onto the ground in the same motion, like it was nothing at all, powerless and deserving of no respect, but it needed to have been done first regardless.

BACK INSIDE THE HOUSE, THE Kid found himself in an old kitchen. Still watching himself even while he was doing it, he thought what an odd place it was to be fighting for one's life; though, in the moment, I suppose anywhere seems odd, depending on your definition. The Kid was scrambling and thrashing about on the ground, trying to kick away so's his feet could find purchase on the polished wood of the floor, but it didn't seem like that was in the cards. The Father still had him round the wrist, and was using the other hand to claw at him, reaching for his things. The Kid was alternating fighting to catch his feet so's he could stand and have half a chance to stop this madness, and then also having to fight to keep that other claw away from his packs and pouches, for all the things he held dear, all the things he might need later and had needed so far.

The thing he needed most, he reached back for that now, getting ahead of himself when he wondered if'n he would be able to use it decently with one hand, but by the time he got round to pull the rifle free he realized that it was one of the things that wasn't there. Instead, he turned just in time to see the little boy pick it up, like a toy he'd found. It was a weird time for a memory to come floating up, but when the Kid looked at the little boy pick up his rifle, he thought of himself when he first got it, around that age. He figured the timeline was similar since the rifle was about the relative size to that little boy as it was to the Kid when he'd first laid hands on it, though the Kid had held it with the awe and respect it was due, not some bauble he'd been given in exchange for a pocket of sweets.

Worse yet was the little girl. Not like the boy, off to one side playing with what wasn't a toy; the Kid was her toy, and she dug her nails into him like she was to see what he was made of. Her fingers burned as they dug in, like when an animal gets a swipe at you, and it's clear your skin weren't designed like theirs, to take a shot like that and stand up to it for more. And like an animal, and damnit all like her Father it seemed, once she got her grip in she didn't let go neither, and before the Kid was about to finally get it in him to yell, the little girl reached her hands for his throat … and that's when everything stopped.

A pair of gunshots sounded from the other room, the door doing little to muffle the echo. As that sound faded and the quiet took over, the children cowered away and the Father froze, and all at once there were tears and sobs and apologies all mixing together.

*I'm sorry. I couldn't help myself,* the Father said. He—the children too—were pulled into themselves like frightened dogs, all scared of the same thing. The Old Man stood there in the doorway, jaw set, eyes glowing—not like the Father's eyes had glowed, no— the Old Man's eyes glowed with cold hatred. A hatred so black and pure the Kid had never seen nothing like it in his whole life and he hoped and prayed he'd never see nothing like it again as long as there were things left to see.

*Come on, kid,* the Old Man said, at the same time he pulled the Kid to his feet. He never took his eyes off the Father. *Don't say a word.* Even with the help, the Kid needed to focus to find purchase on the polished wood of the floor here. Once his feet were set, he reached out for—

*Don't touch anything,* the Old Man commanded.

*I ain't about to leave my—*

And again, before the Kid could finish what he was going to do or say, the Old Man shoved him, hard, toward the door. It was a reprimand that didn't need to be handed out twice, so the Old Man didn't bother to look back to check that the Kid had listened. No, in fact, he never took his eyes off the Father. There was still that same hatred, that same glow. Maybe it was for that reason, or because the Kid still figured himself here to help, that he didn't want to leave the Old Man here.

*I'm sorry. Come on, and let's go.* The Kid meant it more as a statement than a request, but the Old Man seemed to feel the other way about it.

*… Soon enough.*

The Kid had made for the door and took another step before the Old Man had answered, and when he turned back with a mind to not be ignored and ask some further questions, he was already outside.

Now, plenty of folks have found themselves in a room and weren't sure why they'd come in, and the Kid felt a similar thing now, except he weren't sure he'd actually gone outside in the first place … yet there he was. There was no point arguing that he had, in fact, left the kitchen, walked back through that house, gone out the door, and then closed it behind him, since, well, all them things must have been done since that's the reality he found himself in now.

The Kid threw himself against the door, hard, with a mind to get it open, but it was no use. His shoulder hit that fine wood and the Kid realized no matter how much weight he might'a had behind it, that door weren't about to budge, even if his shoulder might. He looked around for something to help in his efforts, since he weren't about to stay out here and leave the Old Man to whatever fate inside held for him, when the Old Man's fate let itself be known instead.

The gunshots from inside startled the Kid, shook him from his previous plan of action and sent him in to a panic. Not a panic to do anything in particular exactly, but a panic like the kind a newborn sets in, just screaming and lashing out and doing nothing in particular exactly. The Kid threw himself at the door again and yelled. Not words, nothing but that primal sound of fear and rage and everything in between. More gunshots sounded in response, muffled by as many walls and doors of fine wood, cutting the sound down more and more before it could touch the Kid's ears. At that second set of gunshots the Kid staggered back a little and collapsed, just sat himself down on the ground wherever he landed, panting, angry at himself and the Old Man and the Father and everyone in between, with no outlet for everything he was feeling, the frustration of powerlessness running roughshod over anything else vying for space in his head. The Kid was left there, breathing heavy, feeling every bit like a frustrated child and resenting that more than anything, when the door opened and the Old Man stepped out.

He physically stood in the doorway, halfway between out and in, but was at the same time somewhere else entirely for a moment. Once the moment passed and he stepped fully outside and closed the door behind him, the Old Man exhaled like he hadn't taken a breath the entire time. It looked as though he must have dragged a weight out with him, draped across his neck, weighing him down more than usual.

*What happened in there?* the Kid had to ask, dreading the answer. So maybe it was a good thing that the Old Man responded by tossing the Kid his rifle, then heading down toward the road. The Kid stayed there for a moment, on the ground with his rifle, and was torn between what he wanted to do and what he knew he was supposed to do. Even he wasn't sure which one he was going to pick until he stood up, and instead of pushing his way back into that house and finding out what had become of the folks inside, he caught up with the Old Man and followed him back down toward the road.

*Y'ain't the first, Kid.* The Old Man was talking before the Kid had even fully caught up. *No one wants to hear it. No one listens. Most of 'em have to learn their Truth the hard way.*

The Kid didn't even get the chance to challenge those suppositions or figure out what he meant or respond, before the Old Man stopped and leaned in close to him, grave. *You're not ready.* And he kept on walking down back toward the road, knowing the Kid would follow close enough to hear the rest. *Go home. You can wonder all your days whether you could'a done something, whether you could'a made a difference. You can tell your stories about how you would'a changed things, if you'd only kept on.* The Old Man snapped one of his holsters shut. *But don't do this to yourself.*

The Kid scrambled for a defense, for a reason, for anything to stand up for himself. *I thought they needed help. What's the sin in that? It looked like ... Well, he just got the drop on me, that's all.* The Kid was working on convincing himself more than the Old Man at this point. *How was I to know he was gonna ...* The Kid weren't even sure what words to use at the end there, because he still wasn't sure exactly what had happened. All he knew is that he was sad, not just with the outcome but with himself.

*Go home, Kid. Don't you worry about it, I'll keep on. I'll take care of this.* The Old Man couldn't believe he was saying this, damn it all. *You got me in this far, farther than any of the others. I ain't gonna turn back from it. I already been on the other side.*

*I'm already ruined.*

*But you … ain't ready.* He snapped the other holster shut, absently. A thing he'd done a thousand times.

The Old Man got quiet now, as he reached under his shirt and found that cross. He closed his eyes as he walked, always kept walking, and mouthed words the Kid weren't sure he would'a been able to make out even if he'd'a heard them. All the time, the Old Man kept walking.

*I'm not stopping. Not now.* The Kid meant it.

*You'll continue to defy me, I have no doubt of that. But there will come a time when you listen.* The Old Man spoke as if it were prophecy. The Kid was sure of himself, as it were, but the Old Man spoke as though the world were sure of him.

And maybe the world was, but the Kid still weren't sure. *Oh yeah? Then what?* There was still a bit of challenge in his words, even with all that had just happened, and all that had happened before that.

The Old Man chuckled, *End of the world, probably.*

But it was nigh impossible to tell if he was joking, exactly. And it didn't really matter one way or another, since in that next moment, something happened. The Kid chalked a lot of things up to "something," since some individual things were odd, or uncommon, or just plain hard to nail down without some little bit of firsthand knowledge. This was one such thing, but worse than any such thing before; neither the Kid nor most people on the earth could have said definitively what it was, though most folks left at that moment would'a definitely knew something happened.

*Feel that?* the Old Man said, as if there was a soul alive that hadn't. It was said in such a way that he wanted the Kid to take it in, to feel it, to remember it, so that he could now be one of the many who had felt it, but the few who knew what it was, when the Old Man looked out far off into the distance and told him.

*He's about to open the next Seal.*

## 10. *Through an Empty Town*

THIS WAS THE MAIN STREET. It had once held so many people and so much commerce that it was as if you could still hear the footsteps if you listened close enough. But you wouldn't be blamed for thinking that was long ago, dismissing that bit of fancy, since now the windows were shuttered and the doors boarded up and everything was so empty and abandoned it might as well have never been anything but. There was nothing now, and now was all there was.

Without man there to hold it back, nature had set about reclaiming its dominion. The dust, instead'a being swept away and knocked off outside, collected up and slowly pushed itself into every little space it wanted, where it would then meet more of itself on the other side. It was beautiful, really—everything these houses and stores and stables had been built from had been the earth's, once, and the earth had done nothing more than come and take back what was hers.

Man was no longer used to such things. Nature scared him, and the natural cycle of things was confusing. Man saw ruination and chaos, set himself to the task of keeping things out and away and holding off the natural order of things, because he didn't see them as being orderly. So when a man—the Kid, in this particular—saw the little street, well, he thought something had gone wrong, instead'a realizing something had just … gone.

*He's here?* the Kid asked, looking at each board on each doorway as though it might be an enemy.

*No.*

The Kid didn't understand. He didn't understand the street, and he didn't understand the Old Man's response. *Then what are we doing here?*

*It's where we need to be*, the Old Man said. He was back to talking in that cryptic way that made the Kid feel like he was being made fun of.

The Kid didn't like that feeling, and he was sick of not being told the whole story, and he had begun thinking to himself at night that maybe all the things that had happened to him wouldn't'a happened quite that same way if'n the Old Man had just told him outright what he meant to say, instead'a spending time like this trying to teach lessons and make the Kid guess and everything else that's infuriating when you're on one side of it.

*Why? If He's about to—* The Kid cut himself off there. He knew what the thing was, but there was more than a big difference between knowing a thing and putting words to it. The words gave the thing power, in a manner of speaking, and the Kid didn't want to give it any more power than it was already gonna have, just being known. *Well, then what are we doing out in the middle of nowhere?* It was a fair question, and the Kid didn't feel like they was gonna be any more out or any more nowhere by him putting words to that. He kicked at the dirt, frustrated, and saw almost how it all started bunching up again right away, like he'd upset an anthill, and nature was just gonna get right back to setting things her way whether he liked it or not.

The Old Man thought a moment, actually put some consideration into what he said next and how he said it. *What He's doing is gonna get done whether we like it or not.* The Kid was about to cut him off, to ask another question, but the Old Man didn't suffer none of it and went right on talking. *And we'll know when it happens, there won't be no mistaking it. And then, in that moment, He'll be revealed to us. Maybe—but only maybe, y'hear—if luck's on our side, and if'n we ain't too far away, we can find him 'fore he reaches the next one. Then, depending how things turn out, we might just have a chance to stop it all from happening.*

The Old Man stopped, right there in the middle of the street like that sort'a thing didn't matter anymore. That, and everything he said, all sounded like defeat, and accepting a fate they didn't have to, and the Kid didn't like a single word of it.

*Well what kind'a plan is that?* the Kid asked, accusingly.

*Yours.*

The Old Man was right, and the Kid shut his mouth, leaving him standing there as well, not exactly sure what else to do. *So we just stop here, and ... wait?* the Kid asked. It was less accusing this time, but only a shade so.

*He'll make Himself known*, the Old Man said, as he smoothed out a little patch on the ground, the same way the Kid had seen him do countless times before.

*Right here?* This time, there was no accusation in the Kid's voice.

*Why not?* the Old Man responded.

*Well, it's the middle of a street, for one.* The Kid looked around, and he saw what he had hoped for. He pointed to a building close by; all boarded up and such, and its sign was fallen, but it was a good bet it used to be a lodging house of some kind. *Wouldn't you rather sleep on a bed, under a roof?*

The Old Man didn't bother to remind the Kid of the last time he'd slept under what passed for a roof, or all the times before that which didn't do him or them any good. None of it mattered. It was human nature to be contrary when presented with something you didn't want to do. The Old Man kept to the matter at hand, said as matter-of-fact as anything had ever been said, *Might miss it.*

That wasn't an answer, as far as the Kid was concerned. *Miss what?*

*I told you. He'll make himself known.* The Kid realized the Old Man was looking off, out at the horizon … where there was a storm coming. And the Kid caught himself looking at it for a while as well. Studying the way the clouds started forming, tightening up around each other, darkening even as they were being watched.

Folks talk about how man has lost his baser instincts, left behind the animal knowledge he's supposed to be born with. With all the tools and reading and songs and everything else that separates man from beast, sometimes important and useful things are forgotten, or written over by new learning, or just plain ignored. But there was no amount of study or art or eating food brought to you by another that could leave a man wondering what was on its way, with those clouds behaving the way they were now. There was likely a deeper lesson in there, and perhaps the Kid could'a thought about it like an old witch would throw bones and tell yer futures, but for the moment, all they did was confirm exactly what the Kid had a mind to do in the first place.

*I'll leave a window open,* the Kid tossed off, joking-like, as he made his way toward the building he'd pointed out.

*You know,* the Old Man said, *might not actually be the end of the world, you listen to me.*

The Kid weighed the Old Man's words—which he'd heard plenty of—with one last glance at those clouds, and moved himself to his new spot.

*How 'bout this. I'm just gonna sleep on the porch here, at least under the awning. That way we're both happy.* The Kid meant it, too. He thought he was being magnanimous, coming to what he considered a compromise. Not that he needed to compromise on where he slept, of course, since the Old Man weren't about to get any more or less wet owing to where the Kid slept.

It must have been a fair compromise, he thought, since the Old Man knelt at the little patch of ground he'd smoothed out. Naturally, the patch was already unsmoothed by the march of the dust and dirt, so there was no real discerning where the patch had been, but that didn't seem to bother the Old Man at all. The Kid watched the Old Man out there with his head bowed, studied him awhile now, and it took some time before he realized what was sitting in the back of his mind, letting him know something was wrong. It was a sight he'd studied every night forever, but this time something was different.

*Ain't you gonna set up them symbols and all your whatnot?* the Kid finally asked. He wasn't sure if the Old Man heard him, then he was even more not sure if he should'a asked while the Old Man still had his head bowed and his eyes closed, and started worrying that he hadn't remembered his manners right... .

... *Don't wanna miss it,* the Old Man said, when he was good and ready. He lied himself down on the ground, curled up, resting his head on his arm. The Kid couldn't help but think the Old Man looked like a child, one who could just up and sleep whatever place he found himself put. He wasn't sure if he was judgmental or jealous of that fact, as he got his own self situated up there on the porch. It seemed there wasn't a good spot to try and get comfortable up here, and he finally ended up in a strange sorta way of sitting, wedged up against the boards that had been used to close up the door to the place, that he told himself he wasn't going to have gotten into anyway, so it was better he'd just decided to stay out here after all. It was comfortable enough, and at least he was under a bit of shelter, and there was less dirt up here, up and off the ground a ways as it was. The Kid pulled his cap down a bit, just off the back of his head so's it could cover his eyes, hoping that he could sleep a bit longer than the sun if he was lucky.

*I'll just be right here,* he said, not quite loud enough for the Old Man to hear, if that's who he was talking to.

IT WAS STILL DARK WHEN the Kid heard a scratching. It was a sound he recognized, old boots shuffling and scuffed over a hard ground. It was the sound that touched him first, forced his eyes to open, and he wondered if it was dark only because his trick with his cap had worked right this time for once. But when he tilted his head slightly so's he could get a better glimpse, the opening let in bars of light that was exactly dawn but before what a man thought of when you used that word, that version of what folks called light gave him just enough to see by.

Someone was walking past, about halfway between him and where the Old Man was still sleeping. The Kid's senses all turned up high at once, reaching out with everything he had to try and tell if there was any kind of threat, but he could have just as easily kept them senses nice and dulled, or just slept through the whole thing, really, since it was clear to see—or hear, for that matter—that this was just a man, shuffling along the ground, sorta shiftless, like he was lost.

The Kid's eyes shot next to the Old Man, to see how he was responding, to see if he took a different view of things. To say it came as a surprise that the Old Man was still sleeping was to do a disservice to surprises; the Kid would never, in a year of guesses, have guessed the Old Man weren't at least gonna be up with his eyes open, maybe even looking at the Kid in that specific "I tol' you so" way he liked to use. The Old Man's response—the lack of, specifically—was oddly reassuring in its surprise. The Kid had grown to trust that the Old Man was far more liable to see a threat in any given thing than he was; he would see threats the Kid didn't notice, and would worry after threats the Kid didn't think they should concern themselves with, even if oftentimes he was proven wrong. It was easy to remember all the times the Kid had been mistaken, and gone inside somewhere he shouldn't, or made a move that in hindsight weren't the best course of action, but there was just as many times the Old Man insisted they keep on and the Kid listened, or the Old Man wouldn't let them refill their flasks at a certain well, or the scores of other times things of that nature had happened, and really there was no way of telling who was right, since once one course is taken, it's not like a man can go back and take th'other.

All that said, the Kid sat up and set his hat right. He wasn't making any particular effort to keep quiet or out of sight, but still the man walking didn't take notice. Just shuffled along, lost, not sure of much. *Sir? You alright there?* the Kid called out, casual like, the way he would talk to anyone from a little town he was just passing through. The man didn't seem to pay him any mind, though a moment or two later he did look back; not at the

Kid, or even at the Old Man, really, even though he'd passed by where he'd been sleeping and so looking back had him looking in that general direction. No, where the man looked back as he shuffled, his eyes found dozens more, just like him.

They was people of all shapes and sizes and descriptions. All in white, all kinda shuffling and walking, but all in a hurry, staggering with what was left of their energy after a long day, still having to keep going. They were spaced out haphazardly, maybe two or three together in some places but many more just by themselves, stumbling here and there. Among them were those wailing and crying out for and after nothing in particular.

But it must have been something, because why else were they in such a rush? What were they in such a hurry away from? The Kid's mind raced, rushing to catch up to thoughts, to put the pieces together, as, in the midst of all that going on, the Old Man went and got himself up and collected his things. He had all the concern of a lady putting away after her tea, as he stood and looked over to the Kid. *Come on, then,* the Old Man said, before he too started walking.

But the Kid needed another moment to take in all the people, and settle all the thoughts he'd rushed and caught up to. *It's happening,* the Kid said, mostly to himself, and that was about as much as he'd been able to sort out.

*Told ye He'd make Himself known.* And with that, the Old Man slipped into the exodus. It was effortless, like he knew exactly where they were gonna be, even with their awkward, lurching movements. The randomness didn't seem so random, to see the Old Man deal with it.

The Kid, to his part, hadn't yet moved. He had just now caught up to the rest of his thoughts, and what had eluded him at first was the most basic of things, something he'd known since he was actually a kid:

*… And when He had opened the fifth Seal, I saw the souls of them that were slain. And they cried with a loud voice, "Dost thou not just and avenge our blood on them that dwell on the Earth?"*

The Kid said the words by rote; he'd known them back and front all the time since he was little. But he hadn't "known" them, exactly; before now they was just words. It was only in the present moment, when he saw all them faces—all that sorrow, fear, all that hatred; there, a dirty child, crying, parts of their cheek and nose freshly burned, agony to look at so's must have been agony to feel—that the words finally meant something. They weren't a mere idea or concept; they was real. They was ideas made flesh. The words had come to life, come to be, come to pass. They were both warning and prophecy. They had happened, were happening, and would no doubt happen again, unless …

*We're supposed to help them … aren't we?* The Kid knew that part of the words, too. The understanding of them. The meaning behind the words—he knew that right in this moment, what the actions were supposed to be. He looked forward, then back, then forward again, and though he knew what actions he wanted to take, should take, he didn't know where to start. There were hundreds of them, everywhere. The first man he saw, the one shuffling, weren't in fact the first, since there were legions ahead of him. And there was no telling where it would end, since the folks coming after—all dressed in white, cresting toward them like a wave—were innumerable as well.

*Nothing we can do for 'em, 'cept what we're doing,* the Kid heard the Old Man say, which should have been impossible since the Old Man was still walking along, weaving between the people like a specter hisself. With the noise, with the wailing and howling, there should have been no way for any other sounds to make their way through, but the Old Man had found the breaks and rests between the noise, and like a composer he inserted his words in exactly the right spaces so they could be heard clear. Still, the Kid wanted to follow, fearing if he didn't move now he mightn't ever find the Old Man again. Worried he would get lost in the sea'a folks, he ran alongside, staying close to the porches and buildings, trying to see above the line'a folks, knowing that it should have been easy to catch sight of the Old Man, not wearing white as he was; he should'a stood out like coal in the snow. The Kid told himself not to panic. Made himself calm. Reminded himself all things worked out the way they was supposed to— that's how he'd been taught at least; it always seemed silly to say it like that, since there was no real way of knowing if it was true or not—and even started to walk himself through the next steps of what would happen if he never found the Old Man again, when sure enough there was that coat'a his, in amongst the sea of white, and the Kid caught up to him pretty quick after.

The Kid was surprised to see it wasn't the Old Man navigating with the expertise of some old river captain, it was the folks walking past who were parting, out of the way, giving room. The Old Man weren't doing nothing, and the folks weren't paying him much mind, what with their eyes all fixated to the skies, staring up, enraptured in their wailing. It was like they was water, simply breaking around a rock without concern.

The Kid was about to suggest moving out of the wave, moving up and alongside nearer the buildings to make the going easier, when he spotted something up where he would have been aiming to go. There was a child, wandering off, wailing in that way a child wails when it's lost and not sure where it's supposed to be, but knows it ain't supposed to be where it is. The Kid watched as the child pulled its way up the steps toward the door of what was likely once a store, and it scratched and cried to no avail there, and sorta wandered its way to the next set of doors covering up what could'a been any old thing, really, and did the same thing.

*She's gonna be left behind,* the Kid said, before he tugged the Old Man's shoulder to point out what he'd seen.

The Old Man seemed unconcerned. *She'll be fine. We ain't got time to worry after that.*

But the Kid couldn't help but look back at the child, who repeated that heartbreaking pattern again. He wanted the Old Man to see it, to understand the child's pain, to want to reach out and help, but sure enough the Old Man just kept on, making his way through the people, almost defiant in his efforts not to look at the child.

The Kid was gonna listen to him and follow, really he had meant to, but he took one last glance back at the child, now just sitting outside one of the buildings, not even near a store, and weeping silently to itself, and the Kid just couldn't go on. He turned back, ran with the crowd a moment before he could slip his way out to the side and run alongside closer to the buildings—much faster this way—to make his way up to the child. He knew he had failed one of the Old Man's tests, as it were, but the Kid told himself it didn't matter at this point, he'd failed so many already the failures started feeling like the normal way of things, and plus was the fact that how come the Old Man gets to decide what the answers are? If the test is whether or not to leave a child alone and crying while the folks tasked with looking after her run away down a street, why not fail that one? Better yet, why let someone else decide the answer, when the Kid himself could just as easy come up with his own, and maybe the rest of them failed that one instead.

*Come on now, little one, let's get you back with—*A scream cut through the air, destroying the last words the Kid had thought to say, and maybe a couple before that too. This wasn't a wail or yell like before, this was a cry of terror. Of ruination. Of destruction and pandemonium and darkness and hatred, and the child jerked away from the Kid's gentle hand—he was just trying to pull her along—and she clawed at the slats covering the closest door, desperate to get inside, bloodying her fingers as she dug her soft skin into the hard wood and the latter came out the victor.

The Kid backed away, startled, unsure what he'd done wrong, more unsure what he should do next, but now most certainly sure he'd failed this test. It weren't never the right way, to have a child collapse, exhausted but somehow still screaming, eyes pursed shut and tears still fighting their way out. The Kid knew he'd done wrong, and the others knew as well. All of 'em had heard that scream, and some of them now changed course. No rhyme or reason to who was selected—or selected themselves— to come, but they moved toward the Kid; ostensibly to help the child, he thought, though he had no idea what that might entail as pertained to him or his safety.

*We might already be too late.* It was the Old Man, and he was next to the Kid, pulling him along. Away from the crowd what was converging on them, away from the child, back in the direction they used to be going. There wasn't anger or judgment in his voice, it was just a fact, just something he thought the Kid should know. The Kid went with him, of course, as he should have in the first place, and he cursed himself for continuing to be defiant and not listening and trying to find his own answers to these tests. He watched as a small group gathered around the child and comforted her. They didn't move to get the child walking again, but instead sat and kneeled as though they would be staying awhile.

One of them looked up and caught the Kid's eye as the Old Man dragged him away. *Why?* the Woman asked him, watching as the Kid was pulled into the night. Her first word cut him deep enough, but her last words stuck with him for a long time afterwards, made him realize the error of so many of his ways, made him rethink his damnable desire to come up with his own answers to the test. Her last words, as he disappeared into the darkness, away from her and her flock, out of that sea of white, into the darkness, she called after him:

*We were going to be saved.*


## 11. A Frozen Lake, Under the Light of a Full Moon

IT WAS JUST OUTSIDE THE edge of the town, down that main street. They came across it fast, like it took no time at all, especially compared to how long it took to get other places these days. It made sense the lake was the foundation the town was built on, and the street designed to get to it easy, for whatever reason a man might need to reach the lake. This time a year it was ice, not water, and it served a different kind of purpose through those long months, though that purpose was long since forgotten, and tonight it served another one entirely.

The ice itself was pristine, a translucent gleaming blue and white and clear all whirled together to make something no man can accurately describe, but at first glance anyone could say that's the color ice is supposed to be. It was sickening, all the more so, given what purpose that pure, clear ice was serving now.

A battle raged, upon and around it. A battle of guns, of blades, of fire that slicked the ice with water before it refroze—making things worse, if such a thing were possible. There was no describing the horrors that were meted out there upon the battlefield, the ice and what surrounded it, there were no words for the fury the men fighting had shown one another. Above, watching, was the storm. The clouds had formed hard and cold like the ice, and they stood watch over the battle…. There was no rain, yet, but the clouds would decide when they would unleash that volley upon the men, making things worse still, if such a thing were possible.

The Old Man didn't wait or watch, he didn't stand at the end of the street and study what was happening; he marched down, meaning in each step. He unsnapped his holsters, his hands ready for what came next. There was no trepidation in his steps. Anxious, maybe, and mad at the distance he still had yet to cover, the steps left that kept him out of the fight, but not cautious.

The Kid was nervous. He slipped on his first step down, excited as he was, paying more attention to the battle so close by, more making sure he would have his rifle at the ready than he was to making sure he took the right steps, and so naturally took the wrong ones.

*Is He here?* There was no hiding that excitement, that different kind of anxious the Kid felt. He had never been close to something of this magnitude, and there was no preparation for it in one's mind, even if they had.

*Somewhere. Maybe. Hard to tell.* The Old Man didn't look anywhere in particular, but kinda took the whole thing in at once, from ice to men to storm. It was all one thing to him. He had his guns out—he hadn't drawn them, from what the Kid had noticed, they were simply out one moment, when they weren't before. *Only one way to know for sure.*

AND WITH THOSE WORDS DID the Old Man charge into the fray—no, "charge" wasn't the right word. That word conveys the wrong kind of meaning; he didn't hurry, he was unfazed by the tumult around him. This was a return to a familiar place. A comfortable place. This was his homecoming, to be at war.

The Kid stayed close; he didn't know what else to do. He fumbled for his own weapon, tried to calm his nerves, tried to keep one eye on the mayhem surrounding and engulfing him. He wasn't sure what he was watching out for … nor did it matter, as it was the Old Man that drew the majority of his attention.

It was strange to watch this gentle soul, whom the Kid had seen on his knees every night before bed, eyes closed and saying private words without moving his lips, undergo such a transformation. Strange to watch the Old Man become a force of nature. A killer. The façade had fallen away, the Truth of the Old Man was finally, here, revealed. His true nature. A costume he'd worn for too long, discarded.

The Old Man's twin pistols moved in harmony, almost of their own accord. He never aimed. he didn't have to—the pistols found their own targets. They never missed. Every shot made fatal. And the sound …

Even with the cacophony of gunfire surrounding them, these stood out. Unique. Overwhelming as a clap of thunder. Just as powerful.

So much so, even the clouds couldn't tell the difference, for as the pistols started, so did the rain, as though the clouds heard his thunder and thought they'd forgotten their own. And when the rain started from above, when the storm arrived, the thunder in the sky was matched only by the thunder on the ground.

Almost against his will, against his better judgment, the Kid followed in the Old Man's footsteps, shadowing him as best he could. He wanted to help. He wanted to fight, to make a difference here. To say afterward that he, also, had a hand in the battle's outcome.

But it was confusing, for through the iron sights of the Kid's rifle, they all looked the same. Everyone on both sides—if there were only two, for there could have easily been more—were too alike. There were no uniforms, no standards, no patches. Skin, clothes, faces, all the same.

He called out to the Old Man for help, asked how to tell the difference, how to identify friend from enemy.

Only the pistols replied.

For down the barrels of the Old Man's guns, a different story was told. Where two men fought, when lightning flashed, there came a revelation:

One, illuminated, bright, beautiful. Goodness, brought to form. The colors of ice, folded in on themselves again. A sight to send a man to his knees weeping with love, and devotion, never to stand again.

The other absorbed the light, as though made of darkness itself. There were no details, no features; it was at best a silhouette. A twisted, horrible outline of something other than a man. Only the eyes shone through—eyes that the Kid had seen before, though from here, he didn't know it.

Thunder rang out from the sky, and that moment was over. It was just two men, now. Thunder rang out from the pistols, and then it was just one.

But more kept coming. From every direction they came, bringing with them their future, leaving behind only carnage, such that it was clear the fighting would never end, here or anywhere else. Even with a thousand pistols, ten thousand rifles, all the thunder of the earth brought to bear, could there be enough to stem the tide?

It was that understanding and realization, come to at the same time, which finally commanded the Old Man's attention. He lowered the pistols and watched. Watched as the rain pounded harder, as the battle continued unabated, as it would for eternity.

The Kid hurried to his side and called out, *What do we do?*

The Old Man watched the fighting, back to seeing everything all at once. *Them in white, they would have gone on, raised up the militias, given us a chance. But you stopped 'em.*

He holstered the pistols as the fighting continued to intensify. The Kid couldn't be sure if one was a result of the other, but he'd be a fool to ignore the possibility.

*And now … all is lost. He's gone.* The Old Man wasn't looking at anything much, now, his eyes mostly glazed over at the blur of what was happening. And as a man approached him from the side, an old axe in his hand and hatred in his eyes, there was a good chance the Old Man didn't see either one of them. There was no time to think or speak, or move, or warn. The Kid's rifle simply moved on its own: shoulder, iron sights, trigger.

**The Call put thunder to shame.** Everyone, from the ice to the clouds and everyone caught in between, noticed. The kick was more than the Kid expected, and no doubt a damn sight more than the man expected. He was shot, writhing on the ground now. Gurgling a hideous noise of a death rattle, as a darkness seeped up and surrounded him.

Now the Old Man was watching—watching the man die. He waited until that darkness finished its duties, then turned to look at the Kid. He studied him, different from all the other times he'd studied him, saw him with his rifle still held tight, aimed at nothing, now. Saw the Kid shaking, breathing fast, which would'a fouled the trigger pull, tears streaming down his face, which would have blurred his vision.

*I shot him.* The Kid almost didn't believe it. He still hadn't moved.

*So ye did.*

*He was coming for you. I saw it in his eyes. So I shot him. I killed him for it.* The Kid lowered the rifle, which was still shaking. He stared off through the rain, looking past the battle and off to nothing, crying now. Tears unabated, like the rain from the clouds. The Old Man knew that feeling. He knew that pain, and the terror—not of what you did, exactly, but of how you felt about it, and what it meant to you, and what was next, and everything else. He knew it all.

*It's horrible. It … How can a man live with himself after something like that?* The Kid tossed the rifle, disgusted with it. With himself.

*Now you seen the other side, Kid. First one tells you everything you need to know.* The Kid turned away from the Old Man's words and watched the battle rage around them. He was no longer a part of the thing, he was a spectator from the outside, taking it all in. He watched all the other atrocities taking place, so close by, and saw himself in each one, saw his actions in each one.

*I can't. I can't do it.*

There was something coming that the Kid didn't notice, but the Old Man knelt in preparation.

*Now you know. You've got no obligation to be something y'ain't.*

The Kid turned toward the Old Man's words now, and in his fury didn't bother to ask why he'd knelt, nor did he notice what was coming. He was too furious, maybe focused on the words, but mostly with himself.

*Stop it. Stop telling me it's okay to be scared. Stop telling me it's okay to be weak. Stop with your pity, and these damn riddles, and just leave me be.*

The Kid's words came down like a command. And in a roar, the Old Man was gone.

## 12. Flood

**WATER RENT THE VALLEY IN two.** Nothing was spared.

The last moment of the battle was captured, frozen in time under the water. The bodies, holding on to their last actions forever now, all hung there, suspended, weightless; the push and pull of the tide coming in and going out at the same time lifted them and held them in place, and nothing there would change for a long, long time.

**THERE WAS ONLY DARKNESS, NOW.** It stayed that way for what would have felt like an eternity, if'n the Kid was even capable of feeling things like the passage of time, what with the condition he was in. Whenever he finally awoke, it was some distance away, in a long-dry sluiceway. Why the sluiceway was dry—as a byproduct of the flood, or any of a number of other reasons—was a mystery that would go unanswered, but the Kid was thankful for its current state nonetheless. It was overgrown and decrepit, a situation which would have rendered it invisible from a distance even in the light, never mind now. When the

Kid finally pulled himself up from the silt, he found himself filthy, battered, and bruised, but he counted on the positive side of things the fact that he was still breathing, and for a good while there as he sat amongst the fine sand, he figured that was the only side of things that really mattered all that much to him.

He reached out a hand with a mind to help himself up, and almost immediately wished he hadn't. Every movement sent a sharp sting of pain through places it had no business interacting with, and he needed to wait awhile and catch his breath in between each one, then steel himself against the pain he knew was coming, and grit his teeth and bite down so's not to yell and curse himself for being weak just to be able to get his feet underneath him. It was twice as long again before he felt comfortable letting his hand go so he could stand up on his own, look about, and try to get his bearings.

*Hello?* he called out, and the words didn't even echo, like the world was letting him know there weren't a single chance anybody was gonna hear him, lest they was standing right there beside him and somehow he'd missed 'em. *Where'd you end up?* he asked again, just in case, and again was met back with a dull, muffled sound like he'd been asking the question into the sleeve of his jacket.

It was a good question, though, since otherwise the Kid had no idea where to go and even less idea what to do. It took him quite a bit of doing, lots of steps forward and even more back, as he pulled himself up and onto one side of the sluice—he chose the way purely on how steep it was, and what kinda purchase he could find on the stray roots and branches hanging down far enough to give him a chance at getting out. It was dark, no stars to speak of, and there was no telling east from west, so he just picked one direction as good as th'other, and he started walking. As he went, he searched aside hisself as best he could, thinking if he'd come this way and ended up here, it stood to reason anyone else might have as well.

*You out here?*

No. No he wasn't. Nor was anyone else. Just the Kid.

He walked long enough that he figured if things were the way they were supposed to be, by now the sun would'a come up, and there would'a been some kind of light for him to get his bearings by. Instead, it stayed dark, the kind of dark that let the Kid know it weren't that the sun was obscured behind heavy clouds or a mountain crest way out that way, where at least the light can peek around corners and find its way to you after a while. This was just darkness.

Later still, and he found himself walking along a well-traveled road. The sluiceway had continued on, but seeing as how there wasn't no water in it, there weren't no reason for a man to continue following, as there weren't likely to be anything of note farther down, seeing as how there hadn't been nothing of that sort farther up. But a road, a well-traveled one such as this, felt like the kind of thing that a man wandering around would follow, and so the Kid had done just that.

There was debris and wreckage everywhere. Old machines, long past usefulness, taken over by the elements, rusted and warped by time and salt and air and everything else that made a mess of things. All this detritus, what used to belong to folks and be the pride and joy of someone at some time, what might have had a name, what used to be a treasured possession, full of memories and with memories yet to make, all this nothing that used to represent everything about life, and now the Kid was the only thing living. He made his way through and between the remnants of all that life, and even though the way he was going took him much longer than if'n he just up and went off to the

side a little there, where the path was clear enough, he decided
it was worth the bit of inconvenience to be close to memories
like that.

And though the darkness did him no favors in all manner of
things related to his travels, when the sun finally came up, the
Kid sorta wished it hadn't. Without warning, one minute it was
dark and the next minute it was bright as day, in the way people
mean when they say such things, and the cool air swapped out
for an oppressive heat that stifled each movement and drained
every ounce of energy. He kept walking through a wide field,
making his way through and between weeds as high as his
chest, that relentless light and heat crushing him like a heavy
stone being lowered one bit at a time. The Kid thought back to
navigating through the ruins of all that old machinery as he did,
and though the going here was smoother—the weeds moved
out of the way more gentle than the wreckages did—he wished
he might'a been back there, what with the darkness and the cool
air and all.

## 13. An Arched Bridge, Over a Ravine

**THAT NIGHT—THE KID KNEW IT was night,** since this time
the sun had gone down properly, so there was something to tell
the difference of—the Kid was crossing over a high expanse of
bottomless nothing. The span across it might have once been
a wonder of engineering, soaring high and supporting its own
weight and all those other bits of trivia that once impressed
people, but now it was just a couple long bits of metal with slats
along the way, and them all broken and rotted.

Owing to that rot, and the fact that those slats weren't exactly
placed at regular intervals, but instead laid out where it seemed

like a man could just barely get from one to the other if he was careful, the Kid had to watch his step. It was slow going across, but would have been fast going down, and being that it was night, the Kid couldn't tell exactly how far the fall would be, but it had that feeling of unending darkness that made him feel like it was long enough to not want to take it.

The low-lying fog that had been surrounding the Kid for most of the night retreated suddenly, like a tide pulling back out to sea. The Kid didn't think much of it in the minute, instead impressed by the view it left behind: a city, miles away, but so big it seemed like he could just reach out and touch it. It was bright, too—it used the proper new lights that could turn on in an instant, rather than the old candles and torches he was used to back home—and its tall buildings shone like beacons, each one a lighthouse, sending not a warning but a warm glow of invitation off into the night sky.

All at once, the Kid was determined to go. It was as good a place as any to start searching in earnest, and there'd be people there. People he could ask around about, people he could talk to. People not just to learn lessons from, or bear the brunt of lessons by, but folks that was living a regular life, and maybe, if'n he was around them, even if only for a second, he could live a regular life too, in that moment.

But in this moment, right now, it was the slats that demanded his attention. It wouldn't take much of a wrong step, a slide of the foot just a little off true, to leave him in a position where he'd better hope that wherever he reached with his hand was the right place, because there weren't gonna be a second chance. And just when he'd felt a bit of pride in finding a good little path along one side of the slats that meant he could take a glance at the city again, it happened.

A rumble, distinct from and opposite of thunder, shook the world. Everything in sight in every direction moved; instinctually the Kid lashed out with a hand for one of those metal beams. It seemed he found the right place, because the iron that had stood so long and so far continued to keep solid, and gave the Kid a chance to find his footing and hold on for what dear and what life he still had left in him. He pulled it tight and wrapped himself as close to it as possible, encircling the piece of cold metal jutting out at such an angle it might as well have been built for him, for exactly that purpose.

Safe for the moment, in the way that as long as a dozen things outside his control didn't go one way 'stead of the other could be considered safe, he looked back to the city, and once again, horrors were visited upon his mind. The reason the fog had rolled back so quickly was revealed—it had all been pulled into the center, of what the Kid didn't know exactly, but tight into one place. And then just as suddenly as it had been revealed, the sky exploded, and fire fell like rain … or maybe it was that the rain was of fire. There was no telling the difference really, nor did it matter, but that was the kind of thought that ran through a man's head when he was witness to something so profoundly devastating.

A THOUSAND SPARKS OF FLINT AND steel fell from above and hit the ground like cannonballs. Under the weight of that flint and steel, of that fire and of that rain, the city was no match. Or, maybe, more certainly it was a match, as the whole of it was burning before it collapsed, and when it collapsed it burned more, spreading that flame out like a flood now, multiplying the destruction as now the flames rose from the ground to meet the ones falling from the sky. The Kid knew he shouldn't watch; such a thing was so terrible, the destruction so total that it would never leave a man's mind. But he couldn't stop looking, and he couldn't stop thinking, so he said:

*And I beheld when He had opened the sixth Seal, and lo, there was a great earthquake; And the stars fell unto the ground.*

The words had been playing over and over again in the Kid's head, and he knew he would never be rid of them unless he spoke them aloud. He stopped there, and he was lost, staring at this disturbing and awful sight ... and he couldn't help but think, too, of the sheer beauty, as the flames of the stars reflected in his eyes, more powerful than all the lights that had been there before.

*And the kings of the earth—* started a horrible, raspy voice, what the Kid heard from close by. Too close, certainly, as the Kid hadn't been paying attention to anything else—leastways anything nearby, which needed the most attention—and hadn't noticed the speaker approach. The Thief now hobbled toward him, closer still, a pile of rags shaped like a man.

*—and the great men, and every bondman ...* the Thief muttered to himself, hoping to make sense of the insanity that plagued his mind, *and every free man, hid themselves in the rocks of the mountains ...*

The Kid held fast with one arm and reached for the rifle with the other, quickly enough to realize his mistake—not in letting go, but in long since not anymore having the rifle.

*... and said, hide us from the face, of Him that sitteth on the throne.* The Kid knew all these words, but he couldn't begin to understand how this one might have known them as well. He backed away, trying to keep something akin to a safe distance, while the Thief kept on.

*... For the great day of His wrath is come, and who shall be able to stand?* And then, as though the world itself was making a point, as the Thief punctuated his last words with an ill-advised

step—not that he was paying much attention before this—the slat he used to be over broke, and he slipped, and he was lucky the one he'd been standing on already could hold his weight for that split second.

His next words were of his own mind—what was left of it—and not recitations of words he'd heard others say previous. His voice was different: calmer, still raspy, but present, rather than somewhere off in the ether. *Most never read the Old Books—* the Thief started, sitting there like a child at play, looking around at the world from this new perspective he'd never considered up 'til now. *How strange to meet you now. Right at the end.*

With that, the Thief gave a little nudge, like he'd hopped up and down just a little while still sitting. It was the way the Kid would have tested a chair to make sure it would support his weight before he tucked in to dinner, but the Thief did it in such a ways that it was like he knew it would break the slat … which it did.

It happened fast enough that had the Kid not already been moving toward him, with a mind to stop whatever insanity he was in the midst of, the Thief would'a fell straight through. Instead, the Kid dived for him, without stopping to wonder whether the slats were gonna bother to hold him, never mind hold them both, and grappled the Thief by the wrist, barely. It wasn't much of a grip, from an even worse angle, and the Kid knew this whole mess wasn't gonna last long.

*Gimme your other hand,* the Kid screamed, as he reached out as best he could without losing what tenuous grip he had on not falling himself. The Thief laughed—laughed of all things, damn it all—and shook his other sleeve, maneuvering it in such a way that the Kid could see just exactly what he was laughing at:

The Thief's other hand was cut off at the wrist, and a piece of broken metal had been twisted in to a hook, nailed through skin and into bone in its place. The whole macabre creation had been wrapped with bandages, but it was impossible to tell how long those had been there, and twice as difficult to tell how long ago the entire operation may have been undertaken.

*Might do you more harm than good*— the Thief said, though he didn't really feel he needed to, having already revealed the more visceral explanation. *Goodbye friend*—

*No, damnit, grab on!* the Kid interrupted, and reached his second hand over the edge, leaving it to chance he wouldn't slip off and be lost forever. Sure enough, the Thief wasn't one to rebuke a second offer—or was this a command?—and he swung that hook of his up, and with impeccable aim that sharp metal dug itself straight through the flesh at the center of the Kid's palm.

The Kid didn't scream. He didn't want to betray anything to the Thief that might upset that man's delicate grasp, so he clenched his jaw and held fast, even as the slat under his foremost foot cracked and started to break, and he had to fight to keep what footing he had, and improve his position at that, as he found the strength to pull the Thief up high enough that the man could get one of his short legs up and on to that broken slat, then reach for the side and get a grip on that metal and hold fast himself before the whole situation went tumbling back and over and gone forever.

Once the Thief was safe, the Kid fell back, his exhaustion from the effort doubled by the pain. His hand was bleeding freely, gouged straight through from one side to the other. The Kid couldn't bring himself to test out whether it could still move or not, the shock of the whole experience still left him holding one hand with the other, staring.

*You're not like him. You don't have the darkness in you. Or maybe just not yet?* The Thief's voice was soft and low, now with a tone befitting the observations of an intrigued philosopher. The Kid was in too much pain to respond, and barely free of it enough to notice in the first place, and so he wasn't sure what to make of things as the Thief rooted through his rags, searching and patting around for something.

*Let me fix it. Least I can do—* said the Thief, raspy again, muttering the way he had before, as he approached with a roll of bandages, old and dirty. That was enough for the Kid to notice, and he recoiled, pulling his injured hand closer as though to hide it, but the Thief's eyes were following the Kid's hand; he was fixated on it now.

*Not as bad as they look—* the Thief said, referring to the bandages as best the Kid could guess, *better than nothing—promise you that—* and before he'd even finished talking the Thief had a hold of the Kid's hand, like he'd gotten his own hand in between the Kid's fingers without the Kid noticing. The Kid had no way of knowing for sure, of course, but he felt like the Thief moved in between the blinks of an eye—he was motionless, and then motionless again, except he'd changed places or moved things around. It would have been unnerving in and of itself, even if this specific expression of that ability didn't result in the Thief now holding his arm.

*Best if you just let me do it—* the Thief said, as the Kid tried to pull away. *Saved me—save you—* The Kid tried to wrench free, but the Thief moved along with him, like the Kid's arm was in fact part of the Thief's body, or vice versa. There weren't no strength to it—it weren't like the Old Man's grip—but instead the Thief was weightless, fast, anticipating or reacting to the Kid's movements almost before the Kid made them. In fact, seemingly without ever letting go of the Kid's hand, the Thief now held a heavy brown bottle, made of old, dirty glass, with a torn label that had long since stopped explaining what was inside.

He did quite a job of balancing it between his body and that contrivance what passed as his other hand, and at the same time as he never let go of the Kid, the Thief reached down and bit to the top of the bottle, and yanked what the Kid then realized was a cork out of the top. It came free with a satisfying plug type of sound, then a hiss that felt ominous as anything, coming out of a bottle like that, especially with what the Kid worried the Thief was to do with it.

*Don't fight—let it wash over you—* the Thief struggled to get the words out, then realized the problem and spit the cork free. The Kid's eyes caught it, that tiny thing, as it caromed off the side of the metal supports and down between the slats, off into the misery of what was below. *Don't struggle—* the Thief continued. *There's no point—medicine, destiny—all the same—funny how that works.*

In the blink after he'd finished speaking, the Kid found the Thief had let go of his hand and taken up the bottle. Now, the Kid felt almost frozen as the Thief smiled. The smile was impossible to decipher, as the subdued madness in his eyes masked what the broad grin might have meant, but the Kid could recognize malice where he saw it, and in this there was none. So he wasn't afraid, exactly, when in the next blink he found the liquid from the bottle already pouring out, over, and into that wound. The Thief laughed—it was something like a laugh—and the Kid jumped a little, not having expected a noise like that to come out of the Thief, certainly not in that moment. And as the echo of the laugh subsided into the maw of what lay below them, the Kid had a moment of peace in the quiet, when he realized the pain had dulled, just a little.

*You fight too hard—only makes it worse—that was His mistake—* The moment broke as the Thief wiped the liquid away, leaving pain to reclaim its place in that wound. *Makes it stronger see—*

*adds to it—the whole world left to burn—* The Thief was back to muttering, as he worked with the bandages. He was an expert with those, wrapping them with both of what he used as hands, each as nimble as the other.

*There's always another way—* The Thief finished with the bandages before he finished with the stream of thoughts, and pulled the last bit of fabric up and to the side, holding it hostage as he continued. *A better way—something to quench the fire, see—you don't have the mark upon you—don't have to protect anyone else from what's inside—*

The Thief seemed almost confused by the evident fact he'd run out of things to say. He tucked the nub end of the bandage under one of the bits he'd already wrapped around the Kid's wound, and satisfied as he could be, let go. Free, finally, the Kid inched back a little, using the moment to test his hand, finally, to see if he could move it. It was all by feel, as he wasn't sure it was safe to take his eyes off the Thief just yet.

*Thank you, I guess,* the Kid finally said, once he'd confirmed to himself it no longer hurt much. He nodded, that part its own little thank you, and in that blink the Thief's eyes were suddenly clear. Lucid. No trace of chaos left dancing inside them.

*Each of us has something to give the world. Something to make it better. Even if it requires a great sacrifice.* The rasp in the Thief's voice was gone, replaced with a clear, resonant timbre that the Kid felt would be more suited issuing forth from a king. The randomness of the words he chose, that staccato, arhythmic way of speaking, all gone. Replaced with the voice of an angel.

*Not the first time I heard that,* the Kid said, after a moment considering it. It didn't seem right to ask about the change, but instead made sense to just talk about the things he was saying now.

*I meant me,* the Thief corrected him. *Hope for me yet.* A deep sigh, before, *Even me.* This was a completely different man than stood before the Kid moments ago. He still didn't quite understand the transformation, and worried what might set it back, so he did his best to keep on their present course.

*Where you headed?* the Kid asked.

The Thief shrugged that metal hook of his, out, off in the general direction of the ruined city. *Nowhere, now.*

*Maybe you should come with me, then. Might be easier, together?* The Kid couldn't believe he was offering that thing, to him. Why would he do such a thing?

*No. No. I couldn't. I haven't done anything to deserve that. Not yet.* The Thief leaned over and sniffed the Kid. Nowhere in particular, not his hand or his jacket exactly, but somewhere sorta in between everything. Odd as it was, still the Kid didn't find any threat. *You go on. I'll hold them off.*

The Kid looked back, suddenly, over his shoulder—there was nothing. He was left confused, again, and as many times as he'd felt like that throughout his life, he never got used to it and he never liked it.

*You still haven't seen them, but they're following you.* The Thief looked right back the same way where the Kid had. *I'll stop all but one. He's left for you.*

*I haven't got a weapon.* The Kid remembered that when nothing made sense, make sense of what you can. And even if he didn't know who he was gonna fight, who they were, or why, or a million other things, he knew what a fight was, and he knew what he was gonna need.

The Thief clasped him on the shoulder with his good hand—as good a one as he had—and looked the Kid in the eye, spoke to him as a friend. *You'll know. Everything's changed now. In the meantime, you must be careful.*

He gave the Kid a reassuring squeeze, then shifted to one side and jumped forward, across the slats. The Kid turned to watch; the movement was powerful and fearless, graceful at the same time it was reckless. The Thief threw himself along the bridge, almost careless in what slats he chose to land on, and yet somehow always choosing right, as he reached the end of the bridge and was suddenly gone.

Alone again, the Kid tightened his grip on that metal bollard he'd been next to, held it tight and didn't move. He was suddenly so much more aware of the howling wind all around him, could see the dancing lights of the destroyed city behind him; if he didn't know better, he'd swear he could feel the heat from the flames on his face. He held tight, and was reminded of his awful wound as the blood soaked through the bandages on his hand, ran down the metal, over, around, and through the slats, then disappeared into the darkness, into the nothing.

The Kid was there for longer than he would have liked, cold from the wind and hot from the flames and surrounded by darkness and light and losing his strength by the minute, and he finally steeled himself, told himself from the inside out he had to keep moving. He didn't hurry, he knew this would be slow going and he would have to be careful, but on he went.

Though it took what he would consider far too long, he crossed the bridge and continued on.

A COLLECTION OF DAYS PASSED, EACH much the same as the last, though the Kid was thankful for that. Memorable days tended to be remembered for the wrong reasons, and the days where he couldn't recount much at all generally made themselves so for no good reason, which was a pretty good reason when you considered the alternative.

There were times over those days—the Kid couldn't make heads or tails of when, or why, just that they happened—where he would be walking, and his head would snap round, almost of its own accord, and he would need to check behind him, stop, pause a second, listen, watch, and make sure nothing—no one— was there. He would walk on for a while, head cocked back just enough to keep an eye on the path behind him, before he would shake it off, belittle himself for worrying over nothing, and keep on forward ... only to find himself repeating the whole thing an hour, or a day, later, for no apparent reason.

Even at camp, in a cold bordering on freezing, he kept one eye back to the way he came. Shivering, he piled damp leaves into a pathetic group, then shook his lighter, trying to find a spark. It yielded nothing ... and even then, knowing that he had a cold night ahead of him, he couldn't take his eyes off where he'd already been, just in case.

The next day, a harsh, sleeting rain came and joined the cold. Each seemed to take pleasure in making the other worse, to the point that the Kid wondered if it wasn't the cold helping keep him wet, or the wet more keeping him cold, and even then, he kept looking back. He scraped at the dirt, made himself a small divot, hopefully to fight against the cold ... but that only made the wet worse, as the rain found itself a friendly gulley, which welcomed it to pool and seep into. It was all worse than before. The Kid told himself not to bother to look back. It didn't matter, and if at this point something—someone—was following him? Well, they could take him. He would welcome it. It couldn't be worse than sleeping in the cold mud.

Another day, he sat up on a large rock, which did nothing to block the cold and just barely less to keep the wet away, but at the very least it didn't make neither of them worse. And he knew no matter how he angled himself he wasn't gonna find sleep that night, but seeing as how he hadn't found much sleep the last few, or the few before that, at the very least things weren't worse. He used a few tough little blades of grass to lash some thin sticks together, forming a sloppy and cockeyed cross, which he set into the ground nearby. There were others he'd drawn into the mud, but they weren't liable to last long, even if the rain decided to pick right now to let up. The Kid wasn't sure if it mattered—he didn't know what the point was in the first place—but he did it regardless, making a little circle around him.

Before he could draw the last few, the Kid looked up, and he wasn't sure if it was the direction he'd come, or the direction he was supposed to go next, but he was sure he saw something. At first it might'a been easy to discount it as a trick of the hard rain, but then the Kid stood, and looked again, and damned if he wasn't sure now that he saw a pair of eyes, piercing through the darkness, staring right at him.

The Kid stood up in the rain and just watched at first, watched as the eyes got a little closer. He couldn't see the face surrounding the eyes, or the body holding the face, so he didn't know exactly what it was, but those parts didn't really matter. He could see the eyes.

*Come and get me, then,* the Kid called out. His voice was so muffled and dampened by the rain he could barely hear it himself, and wasn't sure if that thing could understand him or not even if it did hear. But the Figure moved closer, through the rain, and even at this distance it was barely visible still. The Kid's eyes were having a hard time focusing on it, like seeing it through a haze, like the sheets of rain were making sure to obscure it as much as possible even as it walked. The Kid could see enough to know it looked down, at the circle of crosses—which was still holding up even in the rain, good little things—then looked back up at the Kid. This time, the Kid recognized the look in those eyes. It was a challenge.

*I'm not afraid of you.* After he said it, the Kid shivered unconsciously, and it weren't just the cold. Something about looking into those eyes made the hair on the back of his everything stand up straight and send a tingle down his spine, like his body itself was letting him know it was about to mutiny. The Kid overrode that signal and fear, and he took a deliberate step over the line of crosses, closer to the Figure, stood and stared it down, defiant.

*What now?* the Kid asked, by now sure the Figure could understand him, at least as well as he could understand the Figure. He locked eyes with the thing, and even as it moved closer, and the sheets of rain moved with it, the Kid didn't look away.

*Who are you? Who'd you used to be?* the Kid asked again, seeing as how his last question netted him what passed for an answer, he hoped maybe this one would as well. This answer, though, came as the Figure reached a hand out toward the Kid. It was darkness, as seen through a heavy rain that never stopped, mixed with static from his old, long lost radio taken form. Even just seeing it, the thing felt wrong. It shouldn't exist, shouldn't move, and shouldn't be able to touch the Kid's face, which it did next. This wasn't the studying grip of the Old Man, turning the Kid's chin round in his hand to get a better look at it, no. This was the tenuous reach of a child standing at the edge of a still lake, leaning a cautious finger down toward the water to see if the child staring up at them from under the lake was real.

The Figure seemed almost as surprised as the Kid when its hand made contact, and it recoiled a fraction before it reached out again, touching and feeling, seeing with its fingers like a blind mind.

*You here to kill me?* The Kid meant it, he wanted to know. The Figure pulled his hand back, but kept staring. The challenge in those eyes was gone, replaced with a plea.

*Then what do you want?* After a time, like the Figure was considering what was asked of it and how best to answer, its hand pointed toward the camp, toward the rock the Kid had been using to stay up and out of the rain. It was a general indication of a direction, since the individual digits on the hand were still hard to make out, unfocused as they still looked to the Kid's eyes, but the Kid couldn't think of anything else it might have been pointing towards.

*Thought you couldn't pass the …* The Kid motioned with a foot toward the crosses dug into that mud—they sure was holding up against that rain—and even in the doing so he realized the answer to his own question, and he finally understood. Quickly now, the Kid knelt down, turned mostly away from the Figure but still kept his wits about him, just in case. He quickly dug up and turned over the soft, wet earth, then smoothed it out again, creating a break in the circle of crosses, a little doorway leading toward that stone.

*Go on, then. It's yours,* the Kid said as he stood, and the Figure shifted its eyes toward the camp, and the Kid saw a glint of longing and desire in there, like a hungry man finding a dinner … but through a window in another's home. The eyes shifted back to the Kid, and now they were filled with thoughtfulness and concern. A multitude of information had passed between these two in those few looks, and the Kid knew wherein the concern lay.

*I'll be fine.* The Kid stood off to one side, and the Figure looked back and forth between him and the circle, alternating for a moment, before it took its first fragile steps. Once it had moved fully into the circle, there was a visible relief, and the Figure knelt. It reached down into the mud and clumsily, awkwardly, scraped its own cross into the mud, to replace the one the Kid had removed. It seemed unsure of its handiwork, and when it was finished, it looked up to the Kid, both for approval and also, somehow, conveying a deep thanks for the opportunity.

**THE KID STARTLED AWAKE THE next morning, in the mud.** The crosses were all gone, and carefully draped across the stone was a faded cloak, hung by its hood. The Kid stood up, put aside his confusion at what happened and how he ended up there, and decided there was no harm in picking up that cloak and carrying it with him. Stood to reason if this was all a devious trap, well, it would'a been easy enough to just gut the kid like a fish in his sleep and leave him there to die; weren't no reason to leave a trapped cloak hanging up so nicely on a rock.

Later on, when he was walking, the Kid first appreciated how warm, clean, and dry that cloak really was. It hung just right, never felt like it was in the way and didn't chafe none against the patches of skin it hit through the holes in his shirt. The Kid decided it was best that he overlook the fact that he didn't believe the Figure had been wearing a cloak—wearing anything, really—and decided to focus on the fact that this gift, assuming that's what it was, was a good bit of kindness in a world that was otherwise lacking it. But a warm cloak that sat just right as you walked didn't feed a man, nor did it clean him, and itself didn't make the going any easier, so it didn't prevent the Kid from being starving and filthy, or dragging his feet barely one after the other in exhaustion. But it did have that hood, so at the very least he could pull that up over his head and angle it just right to shield his eyes against the bright sun, and he could push on, in just that bit less miserable a state.

## 14. Through the Massive Trees of a Forest

THICK BRANCHES LOOMED OVERHEAD, CREATING a sense of being reached out at and grabbed for. The Kid couldn't see the tops of the trees, even stripped of their leaves as they were, for their height and density caused them to overlap and combine in such a way that after a few feet it became impossible to tell where one ended and another began.

He walked through that thicket of trees for what seemed like hours—though it might'a been days. With the lack of sunlight he couldn't tell what direction he was heading, and when he looked back it was like the path he'd just pushed through had closed itself back over again, so he couldn't quite tell where he'd been, neither. Still, he pushed on, because there weren't no other choice. When confronted with a maze of never-ending turns and twisting passages, all alike, what was there to do except pick one and stick to it 'til you hit the end, then turn back around and take the next?

Finding his way became a war of attrition, and, as always, attrition was winning. The Kid was starving, and had been forever. He found himself at the base of a tree, digging for the roots; he had no idea why he'd picked that tree and didn't remember kneeling, didn't remember scrabbling at the hard earth with his hands … but sure enough, he was in the midst of doing just that, and found nothing, not that he was totally sure what he was looking for regardless. He crawled, desperate, panting, to another tree nearby, and did the same thing. The hard earth was packed tight and didn't budge much under his hands; he wasn't anymore carrying anything that was worth a damn for the job, neither. Finally, after putting enough effort in that he wasn't gonna blame himself for starving, the Kid collapsed, exhausted.

His breath kicked up little clouds of what meager amounts of dirt he'd managed to move, and through that dusty haze he saw a pair of rabbits, sitting some ways away, almost mocking him with their presence. He was too confused—impressed, even— that there was anything alive in here, to think of all the things he might'a done had his rifle been on his back, how quick he could have brought it round, like he'd done so many times before. And it was almost as if the rabbits had heard that thought, for a split second after it flitted through that haze of dust, they scampered off, disappeared behind another of the infinite, identical trees, and the Kid could do nothin' but lie there and watch them go.

Then he saw something else, though at first he couldn't quite make out what it was, exactly. So he stayed where he was for a moment longer, the way you don't wanna move when the light reflects off the water just right, and makes you feel like you're seeing a picture of something, but you can't quite place it. He tilted his head against the ground, just a little, to change his angle, though he was still looking just over there, where the rabbits had been. And finally, it revealed itself: the branches were twisted, reaching not into a chaotic mass of clawing digits, but into a recognizable shape. It seemed unnatural, like they were posed that way, but the Kid had no way of knowing if that were the case, and if it were, how long a thing like that may have taken to do, and for what reason, but he knew for certain what he was seeing now: it was a cross, clear as day once he could see it, and it beckoned to him.

He forced his knuckles against the ground to give himself just that little bit more, slid a knee under so as he couldn't just give up and let himself back down again, and dragged himself to his feet, one pathetic piece at a time. He never took his eyes off that cross, because he wasn't sure if that strange association of branches would look the same from anywhere else, and he was terrified that if it left his sight for even a moment, he would never find it again. For what it was worth, as he got closer to the place, whatever he saw in those branches moved again, and instead of a barely recognizable shape in the twisted branches, he saw what could safely be described as a path, a little different from everything around it, that seemed as good a way as any to go. So the Kid pushed through, deeper into the forest—as far as "deeper" meant anything—and things felt different, finally. There was moonlight, what come through the tops of the branches in spots and slivers, just enough to see by. The branches didn't cling together as tight, one didn't hold on to the next for dear life so much, and as they thinned out and the Kid could see up ahead a little better, he spotted something.

It might have been a man. It was a figure about the same size and shape, give or take, though there was something missing. At this distance and with this clarity of light, the Kid couldn't quite make out the particulars, and so's in an abundance of caution, he froze, hoped what might have been a man hadn't spotted him yet.

The Kid twitched involuntarily when what might have been a man finally moved, though it didn't step; it swayed. An unnatural, awkward movement that all at once made the Kid realize what was missing, what was missing from the whole of a person and left this ersatz figure he saw now before him.

The feet didn't touch the ground, but just barely. You couldn't fit a blade of grass between the toe of its boot and the dirt, but there was no mistaking that what might have been a man wasn't standing, but hanging. With a half-step closer, a shard of moonlight revealed a rope, long and taut, strung up from one or more of the myriad branches intertwined above. The Kid moved closer, and it was as if his own footsteps set in motion a complicated set of gears and mechanisms, for seemingly each step forward caused what might have been a man to sway a little more, to rotate with eerie smoothness, like the shadow on a sundial. There was a sack cloth over its head. The Kid got closer, moving quietly as though not to disturb anything else, but before he was near enough that he could decide why he'd come over this way in the first place, he noticed the rest.

Higher up, in another tree, was another figure. Another rope, another sack cloth. In what was a vicious mockery of how claustrophobic the trees had felt just that little while ago, they were now spread apart and reached out far and wide, but only then to make room for yet another body, another rope, another hood. The Kid stepped back, looked up, and looked around him, finally taking in the totality of the situation. There were thousands: hanged men, women, maybe a few weren't much more than children. Some were higher than others, but that seemed owing to the randomness of the trees and their branches, and not to some mastered plan of what used to be who now belonged where. All the necks was stretched the same, though some were fresher, while others had rotted so long they were barely more than bones.

As the Kid turned and looked and took it all in, he realized that even behind him, there were more. Did he really walk right underneath them all without realizing? That may have been the more shocking of the two revelations; how could he have missed such a thing? And what was he so focused on that he could?

Questions like that had no answers, so there was no reason to stay and search for one. The Kid backed away, being careful not to touch anything front or back, and weaved his way around to where a path seemed to have opened its own way up, almost pointing itself out to him, and he decided to head that way— what choice was there?—as cautiously as possible, as frightened as he was. Where he passed that closest tree, where what might have been a man hanged with a sack cloth over its head, the Kid didn't notice, but there was a cross carved into the wood.

## 15. Deeper, Where Was Found a Clearing

THERE WAS A HALF-DOZEN FOLKS sitting around a low fire, talking and laughing. There were hints of music, but maybe that was just the light and lilting way they spoke, giving the air a bit of a melody, songlike, especially when nothing like that had been heard for some time. They was all carefree, which itself was a word what had gone so long without use it had all but lost its meaning, but one look upon this crew and it was clear that word needed to be brought back into full usage and hollered from the mountaintops. The folks were surrounded at the edges of the clearing by their tents—worn by harsh weather, but well-kept and tidy, their ropes strong and taut though they'd clearly been set here a while. All the tents were made of sack cloth.

In the midst of a lively conversation which may have been going for some time prior, one of them suddenly stopped, shocked, when they noticed something at the edge of that clearing. That notice instantly stopped the others, and that whole conversation died a quick death as the rest turned to look: the Kid stepped just into the edge of the firelight. He stayed back a comfortable distance, minding his manners, and pulled his hood back to show clear his face.

*Sorry, folks. I don't mean no intrusion,* the Kid said, obsequious, doing his best so's not to rush any of them to defense. They weren't worried, it didn't seem; instead, all their eyes turned to look at the one amongst them.

*What brings you here, my sweet darling?* The Dowager was old, but the kind of old that brings power stead'a frailty. She was proper, held herself in the way of people from a different time, regardless of what time she was in at that moment. She was the type that made you hurry to pull your hat off and half-bow as you spoke to her, like she was doing a great service by letting your words reach her ears, and that was exactly what the Kid did before he spoke.

*Not sure, if'n I'm being honest with you, ma'am. I got lost coming through the woods.* He half-heartedly indicated back behind him, as though there were any question which woods he'd meant. *I don't mean any harm. Was mainly looking for a sound place to sleep.* He couldn't help it, but his eyes traveled over the empty plates, and a stew still bubbling on their low fire. There was no hiding the hunger.

*… Maybe a bit to eat, if you've any to spare.* Again self-aware and self-conscious, his hands darted here and there, trying to check all his pockets at once. *I can pay. Or trade?* He was shocked to reach into one of those pockets and pull out the lighter—he was certain it was lost along with everything else, mostly since he'd looked specifically for it a dozen times or more and specifically in that pocket each time. But here it was, now, and true to his word he offered it out in trade.

The Dowager smiled; it was warm, welcoming, like your family happy to see you outside after a long trip back home. It was disarming, stealing the Kid's worries away. *We ask nothing in return. You are welcome here, my dear. You are one of us.* After her words settled, she motioned with a hand. Somehow, it was meant both to let the Kid know he could put the lighter back—which he did—and also so's to have one of the men move aside and make a place for the Kid. The apprehension returned suddenly, and the Kid stopped after taking a step forward, as caution roared back to life in his mind.

*You folks ain't* ... Well, now, the Kid wasn't sure how to put this exactly, since there weren't no good way of putting it.... . *That is ... What happened out there? With all them in the trees?*

As the words of his question died in the air, so did the rest of the noises. It seemed even the fire stopped crackling, as once again all the eyes turned to him, everyone in that circle watching, wondering why he'd ask, and what he was aiming to learn.... .

*We do not concern ourselves with the goings-on in the trees, little thing.* The Dowager's voice was naturally sweet, calm and understanding without trying. No motive behind the words; nothing but kindness. Even the most hardened, concerned, anxious of men couldn't help but rest easy hearing it. *Why would we? We have everything one needs, right here. Look around you: there is warmth, food, companionship.*

She looked out past him, into those very trees, and shuddered. Maybe there was something practiced and polished about the behavior, as though she'd done it so many times it just looked natural, or maybe it just was what it was. *What is out there but rancid thoughts and desires, and the horrible actions of man? Whatever punishment was delivered unto them ... it was no doubt deserved.* It felt genuine. It felt like she spoke from the heart, from deep in her soul, that this was the first time she'd been asked these questions and she'd been responding with a fierce passion. *Pay them no mind,* she said, finally, and motioned for the Kid to sit.

Like a fool, he did. And before he could think why he would be a fool for accepting, he'd been handed a bowl of stew—there was meat in there. Real meat. A few pieces put all together to maybe the size of his palm; a feast even in the best of times, never mind compared to what he'd been through as of late. And there was a huge chunk of bread, which was seemingly waiting for him, though he couldn't spot the loaf it had been torn from. Maybe the rest had already been ate, and they just had this bit left over ... but what did it matter? It was food, and they'd rightly offered it to him. It was his first proper meal in he couldn't remember how long; the smell itself was enough to make him forget his manners.

It wasn't until a blanket and some new clothes were laid beside him that the Kid remembered his manners again, and suddenly looked up from the empty bowl. He was embarrassed, so much so he didn't think to question where the clothes had come from, only in that moment was he so overwhelmed by the kindness that had been shown to him, offered up so willingly, with nothing yet asked in return.

He struggled to find the words, confused and thankful and wanting to square the balance and make things right all at once, but the Dowager cut him off before he could speak; she weren't hearing none of it. *Hush. Before you say a word, I know what you're thinking, and you can hush. Those are gifts, and we're happy to provide them.*

True to her words, the others had continued on talking and singing, happy to be there, happy to have him. There was something so comfortable about the whole thing, it made the Kid feel like he was among friends, as much as they were with each other. So much so that even when the Young Woman came and sat down nearby, and inched closer as she talked, it didn't make him feel awkward or shy or none of those things he normally felt.

When she spoke, her words came out in a soft, rhythmic lilt, like they were part of a song. *So wur d'ya come from?* she asked, like it was the most important question the Kid had ever heard.

*I … To the west. Thataways, I think.* It was hard for him to concentrate, and he was a bit confused at what direction, and the which ways and wherefores were impossible for him to call to mind. It was odd, since those kinda things didn't use to pose any difficulty for him … but again, he came up with excuses. Maybe it was that the Young Woman had such a warmth about her, in the way one could tell she was kind and giving and thoughtful to everyone she'd come across. Maybe it was the way she smiled, so's you could tell it was a genuine delight in what she was thinking, rather than a way to disarm you and make you think she was happy. Or maybe it was the way her eyes studied you, really wanted to know what it is you was up to and what you was about, but there weren't no judgment in it; it was all about understanding you as a person, because she liked people, and she liked you. Maybe it was all that. Or maybe it was something else, that the Kid couldn't quite put his finger on. But before he could really think on it too much, and crack through that façade and study the pieces enough, once again came that voice. That disarming, melodic voice.

*Ooh, is't pass the river?* she asked, and the Kid once again couldn't concentrate on anything except answering, and all those other concerns got pushed off one way to the side.

*There was a river, yeah. I remember that,* he said, but even that was a struggle, because if he was being honest, he wasn't quite certain if he did remember it, or if he was just saying that to be cordial.

*I don't remember much. Dun'need to. We're safe here.* And the Kid realized he'd been starting to feel the same way—he didn't really have to remember anything, since what exactly was there to remember? And if he could in fact remember it, why should he bother? Why not take on what was here, and not think of nothing else, and not ask questions?

*What about the ...* the Kid started, but there was a clash in his head when he realized both he shouldn't be asking such questions, and at the same time realized he couldn't quite think of the end of the question he'd started to ask. Instead, he gave up, and ended with ... *Guess it doesn't really matter.*

*Good*, the Young Woman said, emphasizing that simple, single word with a casual touch on his wrist. Her hand radiated warmth, more so even than the fire.

IT WAS SOON DOWN TO embers. The Kid slept, satiated and warm. The fire had served as a blanket, keeping him protected not only from the elements but the world itself. Normally, sleeping out on the road as he'd done so many countless nights, any number of uncommon or unexpected sounds or tricks of the light have a way of waking a man up. Normally, if'n there was a shadow out there amongst the trees, the mere hint of such a thing would snap the Kid wide awake, alert, and would keep him in such a state long after he'd kenned it were only a bird, out late past when was appropriate, or any number of other harmless things what dwelt in the night.

But this time, he didn't notice. The shadow in the trees meant nothing to him, still lost as he was in the dwindling warmth and light of the fire. The thing moved closer—no, moved weren't the right word, since it never moved. It was simply closer, nearer than it was before. And somehow, even as the last embers of that fire died down to nothing, and no more light was given off, there was still a shadow, above the Kid, staring down at him.

It watched a moment. Then … gone.

The Kid slept, undisturbed by a rustling just off yonder that any other night—in fact, every other night—would have awoken him. Even as a sharp cry was choked off—not so soon that the Kid wouldn't have, or shouldn't have, noticed—the Kid slept on. This was the kind of sleep men wished for; deep, without a care, no concern in the world. They wished for that kind of sleep only because there should be nothing in their world so's to wake them, and cause them strife, and not because they simply weren't aware of the world burning down around them as they slept through it all, oblivious to the destruction.

Everything that should have woken the Kid kept on happening, right up through a heavy thud, the sound of something hard against something soft, a sound that came again, then a break, then again, its few repetitions creating a sickening rhythm, were one to be aware enough to hear it. The last thud sounded like a relief, like whatever was getting hit was just happy to be free of it all, and it had given up more than it'd been broken.

When the quiet started back up, it wasn't the quiet of relief, but the quiet of tension, of anticipation of something else yet to come. And sure enough, it weren't long before again there was a shadow looming long over the Kid, but this time something was different. The shadow moved wrong—in that, it moved at all rather than not moving. It was a different shape, it was made of different stuff, and this time, finally, now finally, the Kid's eyes snapped open. He didn't move—maybe it was that he couldn't, but regardless he didn't—but all he needed was those eyes to be open, so's he could see the Dowager, kneeling above him now, staring down upon him with a visage of pure disgust battling with rage.

*Cursed be you, to bring one such as He upon us!* she spat her words at the Kid, who didn't have the beginnings of an idea what she was talking about, and no time to ask and get clarity, before there was a sharp jerk, and the whole of her body were drawn up at an inelegant angle, into the air.

It was then that the Kid's senses came to their senses, and he noticed the source of her trouble: a noose cinched tight around her neck, and now she hanged from it, th'other end of the rope on an overhanging tree. She kicked and flailed, spasming wildly; she, like any other creature what walked, swam, or crawled, didn't want to die when it came right down to it.

See, death is a strange thing; dying even more. It is the one thing we all have in common, yet no one knows a damn thing about it, most of the time by choice. We avoid the thought of it, avoid learning about it, and when it comes close, we avoid studying, as though knowledge of the thing will catch inside us and grow, bringing us closer to it, or maybe making us more likely to take the thing upon and into ourselves. The Kid watched this one to the end, still without himself moving, and the whole business was over faster than he might have imagined. A shooting was one thing: one minute there was life, the next death. This was something else entirely, with the blood and the breath kept from a person, and all at once every thought and every action all focused on the one most necessary thing, and the panic set in which served no purpose and only made things worse, and it seemed like everything happened both at once and stretched out over an eternity, and the Kid was still looking, as though he was waiting for the next step in the process, when he heard a familiar voice:

*Been lookin all over for ye.*

The Kid barely had enough time to bring his focus back, when, with a rude clunk, his old rifle landed next to him.

*Ye might need this, still.*

And still before the Kid could process yet another new piece of information and formulate an understanding and response, he was yanked to his feet—not far from the rough treatment doled unto the Dowager only a moment ago, though it felt like a lifetime—and he once again found himself looking into the eyes of the Old Man.

*You're alright,* the Old Man said. It was dismissive, not a question but a statement, and after he'd made it, he left the Kid and moved off. The Kid was shocked, at the appearance and words of the Old Man, and also, once he'd looked, at the state of the camp: the tents, once well-tended and decorated homes, were left torn and collapsed, with the clear outlines of bodies shrouded underneath, and the oft-mended fabrics now soaked through with blood. There was something more final about their fate, frozen to the ground as they were, compared to the Dowager, still swaying above his head, the slow rocking giving the appearance of movement, and therefore life.

*… The hell did you do?* the Kid asked, as he searched for where the Old Man had gone, and then sighted him rummaging through the meager belongings what used to belong to the folks what used to belong here. The Old Man kept on crouched down as he was, as if there weren't nothing the Kid was doing to hear or to see.

*Tell me what's going on, damn you!* the Kid yelled, louder this time, more forceful, and along with the words the rifle aimed itself—that well-practiced movement came back to the Kid as though it never left. He hadn't even realized he'd done it until it was done; he hadn't time to think about if it'd been a good idea or not, and it didn't matter much to do it now, as there was no undoing it. At this point, all that was left were to live with the consequences of what came next.

And what came next, once the Old Man noticed where the Kid was pointin' that thing, was the Old Man standing, leaving behind what he was rustling through. He locked eyes with the Kid, took a series of deliberate steps, over and between the bodies and wreckage all around him without ever looking away. He didn't stop until the end of that rifle were right up against his chest, and he kept his eyes on the Kid, never blinking.

*Put it down,* the Old Man said, in that old way he'd spoke, where it was less a statement or request and more a command, and what's more a command the Kid would never have dreamt of ignoring before … but times were different. The Kid reset his grip, determined now in his course of action, and convinced of the righteousness of his stance.

*Not until you tell me just what the hell is going on,* the Kid said, and he meant it. He thought he meant it, at least, until the Old Man answered what the Kid didn't even really know was a question.

*I know where He is.*

It took a moment for the Old Man's words to settle in the still air, like they was dust kicked up from a gust of wind. They were powerful words; their meaning played back and forth across the Kid's mind, giving him ample time to absorb the nuance and meaning. It was everything he'd fought for, everything he'd wanted. It gave value to and made sense of all those long nights and hard days and every bit of pain and sorrow since he was little. It was terrifying and exciting all at once, and the Kid was still taking in the totality of the lifetime those words represented when the Old Man spoke again.

*You put that rifle down, and we'll go see this through.* There was a deadly pause before, *You don't, and … well, we'll just see.*

It would have been a tense moment if the outcome wasn't already foregone and done long before the Kid lowered the rifle. Turns out the Old Man's command still had some power to it, even if it took a minute to make its way through to the Kid this time.

*These were good people,* the Kid said, indicating the camp around them, fighting back a sudden wave of emotion as he realized exactly what he'd just woken into. *They helped me. There was laughing, and singing… . Damn you, when was the last time you heard music? They were happy.* The words came out in a rush, and the Kid held out a hand to stop the Old Man from walking away, instead forcing him to answer to what he'd done, as though any explanation could make what had been done all right again.

*You don't know what they were. Think all them folks out there in the trees were accidents?* The Old Man shrugged the Kid's arm away, his action as dismissive as his tone, and went back toward some of the rations and whatnot was still seen here out in the open.

*I don't know what you're talking about,* the Kid replied. It was honest and genuine, that much was clear, and the Old Man didn't need long to study him and realize:

*Then they got to you, too. And you would'a ended up no different had you stayed.*

The Kid needed another moment to think, to harken back on his memories and ask them just what the Old Man might have been talking about, before he spoke. *How do you know? How do you know what they wanted?*

*What I tell you about fire? Draws 'em in, like bait.*

This time, the Kid remembered the reference, and was quicker to refute. *I'm not … one of those things.*

*To them you were.* The Old Man cocked an elbow at the Dowager, now done swaying in the tree, finally looking proper dead. *Whatever you see when you look at them, what do you reckon they see when they look upon us?*

The Old Man got closer to the Kid again, not to make his point, but to tug on the cloak he still wore, feel the fabric. Which, in a way, was making the point as well. *You kill this one?* the Old Man asked, and it was his turn to be genuine in his question.

*Didn't have to,* the Kid replied, proud—this memory was seared deep in his brain, and he would never forget it. He knew it weren't how the Old Man would've dealt with the thing, but that didn't matter; in fact, it was the first time he felt he'd done the right thing, unquestioningly and unapologetically. It didn't matter what the Old Man thought—even when the Old Man got closer still, stood up, and again looked him in the eyes. It was just as he'd done when they'd first met, the same as the Old Man had once done with the pig, the same way the Old Man studied everything he saw and wanted to see more of.

But it was different, this time, when he studied the Kid. He saw something he'd not seen before, something that surprised him, the answer to a question he didn't already know. Finally, the Old Man stepped aside, and pointed to something across the clearing and through the trees: there was a path, out of the forest. Plain to see now that it'd been shown, but easy to miss—impossible not to miss—otherwise. The Kid kept his eyes on it, so's not to lose the placement, even as the Old Man spoke.

*Now, son, I tell you this, and I tell you honest: if you lost the fire, if all that is outta you after what you've seen and all you've done, you ain't gotta go no further. Ain't no one, least of all me, gonna cast judgment on you if you turn off this path.* The Old Man let those words sit. He gave the Kid a chance to consider, to listen and hear and truly understand, before he kept on. *But this is your last chance. All that's happened afore now, only step that matters is the next one.*

With those words came the first rays of the rising sun. The cold light made mockery of the scene around them; at least before there were only silhouettes and outlines of terrible things, but now they were clear, laid bare to see. But with the awful and the calamitous also came the good, the hope of the pathway ahead, clear now to see, to know that even if the Kid looked away he would never lose it again.

*You done runnin' from what's waitin for ye?* the Old Man asked, with finality.

The Kid knew the Old Man weren't lying; there were no judgment or anger, no leaning one direction or the next. The Kid was free to choose; for the first time, completely free. And so he stowed his rifle, and he locked eyes with the Old Man, to prove his determination to him as much as to himself, and he left off through the trees and down that path, into the light and into whatever was next. The Old Man watched him go.

Once the Kid were out of sight, once the choice had been made and couldn't be changed, the Old Man reached a tired hand up and over through the collar of his shirt, and pulled out that old cross of his. He pulled it up, straining to the edge of its simple leather thong, and put it to his lips, where he whispered, almost inaudibly, *I'm sorry,* before he snapped the cross free, kept it tight in his hands, and followed the Kid.

## 16. Ruins, More Than Ancient

FOREVER AGO, THIS MIGHT HAVE **been a walled city,** high on a plateau, raised up and overlooking a broad expanse of something wonderful. The capital of what passed for a sprawling metropolis in its time, home to vibrant culture and society with customs and beliefs, where families grew and expanded and learned and grew some more, and some folks felt pride in what it was, and others wanted for change, and sometimes you saw the same folks every day for years and then never again, and once in a while afterwards you couldn't help but wonder what might'a become of them. But now, not even memories was left, since nothing that would have, or could have, remembered it was in any state to do so.

Nothing except a great church, carved from a solid block of stone that seemed like it came up from the plateau itself. Atop the church was, or had been, a great golden dome, now collapsed and caved and sitting at such a precarious angle one might wonder if it weren't about to fall farther, if it hadn't been there, like that, for uncountable lifetimes already.

The Kid stood, truly struck with awe, at the thought and wonder inherent to all these things. He barely heard the Old Man's words as he pushed past, headed up the spur toward the church.

*Every night. Every night I prayed to never have to see this place again,* he said, and the Kid was then struck more, with his understanding of the Old Man's plight, and of the questions that flooded his mind.

*What's He doin in there?* the Kid asked as he followed, marveling at the details he could make out as they got closer. At each subsequent distance more details were made clear, and more understanding of the care and time and effort that'd went in to such an edifice. And even if this were only one building up high on the plateau, and up high on the plateau only stood above and central to the great plain it overlooked, the Kid couldn't stop his mind from thinking of all the lifetimes that had played out, right here, in the shadow of these mighty walls.

*Hiding*, the Old Man replied, with no such wonder. He approached the building with a disdain bordering on disgust, like a man just washed up, now returning to learn that someone's found a chest-high mound of offal what needs clearing away and there's no one else to handle it but him.

*From what?* the Kid asked, realizing that even as he posed this second question, the sudden arrival of twenty, or fifty, more questions in his mind meant his curiosity about this place, about what had happened, would never be sated. So instead, he decided to focus on what was happening, and what they were doing in the moment, and let everything else fall to the wayside. *What on earth would He be afraid of?*

The door of the place had long since crumbled to dust, but the Old Man stopped at the threshold like it was still there and was closed to the both of them. He looked back to the Kid, and very pointedly didn't answer, but that itself was answer enough.

Inside was breathtaking; beauty shone through amongst the destruction. The Old Man took no time, no consideration, took nothing in. He marched down a long, narrow hallway, past a facing pair of windows—stained glass—that had somehow survived, intact, all these years. Therein were captured images of great heroes, all standing guard, facing out to hold their enemies at bay.

In between them all, the Old Man stopped. He was aligned with an inlay of polished silver, what should have served simply as a highlight on the shield of a powerful man. It was so small as to almost be unnoticeable, but the Old Man couldn't pass it by. It was not curiosity that froze him, no; he knew what he would see when he looked. But he would look, there was no question of that. And when he did, there was no reaction. He studied himself with the same cold stare with which he studied everything else. The Kid, watching from one end of that long hallway still, knew how terrible the moment must have been.

*What do you see?* the Kid asked as he got closer, hoping that if he stood just right, maybe he would see what the Old Man did, though his own thoughts of what he might see made him want to retch.

*… Him.* The Old Man's response stopped the Kid; there was no want left for him to look. Instead, his own interest and morbid curiosity were replaced by compassion, a sadness for the Old Man and a want to make things better.

*Once we kill Him, would that be gone?*

*No. Only make it worse.* The Kid didn't even really understand the totality of the Old Man's reply yet, but what he did understand was devastating.

*So then what do we do?* The Kid wanted to help—it's all he wanted—and he couldn't bear the thought of not being able to, having no power over the situation, and leaving the Old Man in any state similar or worse to what he was experiencing now. The Old Man, though? He always knew it would come to this:

*Kill Him.* There was finality in his words, and the Old Man could finally look away and walk on. He unsnapped those holsters as he did.

The Kid followed, passing unsure and unsteady through the hall. He knew, of course, he had to look over at that mirror. He had to know. He was coy with his glance, as though a short peek— like a gopher comin' up out of its hole to make sure nothin' was around before it headed out for the night—would make any difference from staring full-on and taking that good long look. Neither mattered, since his reflection was just that same old face he remembered, everything just where he'd left it, nothing else worth mentioning. The Kid couldn't tell if he was disappointed or relieved, but either way he readied that rifle of his, and he kept on after the Old Man, since after all that'd happened this wasn't the time to be left behind.

Up ahead was the stone door of a vault, its macabre etchings visible even from the distance the Kid approached. He'd seen those unrecognizable letters before, and he would never forget them, regardless of whether he knew what they represented. As much as there was to take in about the door itself, the Kid's main focus was on the Old Man, who was leaning ever so slightly against that door, tracing his hands across the stone, feeling those letters, like he was remembering them, somehow. He pushed, gently, against the door—his hands barely a whisper— but still the stone moved, ever so slightly.

When he saw that, the Kid rushed ahead, wanting to help, wanting to be a part of what he knew was the deciding moment. He threw himself against the stone with abandon, ignoring just how cold it was—unnaturally cold—and strained and stressed with every muscle he had. Even then, the stone only began to grind, the ease of the Old Man gone, this simple thing turned into a Sisyphean task by the Kid's presence, which should have made the whole thing easier.

He was left exhausted, but the Kid had "helped" create an opening, just big enough. Outward came rushing a dark air; it was burnt, musty, and it hit him like a fist that somehow connected with his whole body all at once. The Kid had to hold on to the stone, the thick, cold edge of the door, to stop from falling over, to stop himself from running away. He took a deep breath to try and settle his racing heart, and risked to peer inside, tried to give his eyes time to adjust, to search out and find anything that might have been hidden.

But instead, from below, from that impenetrable darkness, came an inhuman howl. The aural manifestation of pain and sorrow and rage, collected and combined and expelled all at once. It was a short, sharp noise, un-reproduceable and unexplainable, and no one that never heard it would know what it was like, but anyone who'd heard it—that noise or any like it—knew it was inside them forever and they would never forget it. It was a cry you'd hear at night, alone, for no reason at all except the darkness wanted to keep you for just that one extra minute before you left it behind, or goodness didn't have as firm a grip on you as it thought, and the evil wanted you back. A man'll only hear that noise—that true noise—once ever in his life, and no other time matches up. Plenty have heard something similar, wondered if that was it, and blessed be to them if they never find the truth. But if they're later so unfortunate as to hear that noise—that true noise—they will know that everything prior had stood as bright beacons of light against the true sound of darkness.

And this sound cut through the Kid, pierced him like a dagger, straight through and out the other side, and that passing changed him. He took a step back, trembling, and his next words came out on their own, like the dagger had cut them free. *We can't do this.*

The Old Man watched it all happen—a passing moment he saw take a lifetime—but he already knew. He had always known. From the first day he'd taken the Kid's face and looked him in the eyes, studied him, cold, he knew.

*Prob'ly for the best,* the Old Man said. The noise never stopped, but it wasn't piercing anymore, and the Kid could hear the Old Man just fine.

*No. You listen to me. This isn't fear talking. There's a better way.* And the Kid meant it, too. That dagger had brought him not just trembling but some understanding, and suddenly he knew something, too. Or maybe he just thought he did. Maybe he was mistaking certainty for knowledge, but maybe it was both, this time. But even as that noise continued—that damnable howl— he heard something in it, and he knew.

*Not for me,* the Old Man said. He was still staring into the darkness, so the Kid reached for him; maybe it would help, maybe he was caught in the darkness and needed help to come back out—but on the cusp of grabbing him, the Kid's hand began to burn, the heat instant and impossible, and he instinctually pulled away. The Old Man didn't notice. He never turned away from the darkness.

*Whatever ye do, don't look. Not 'til it's done. And remember this, above all else: He only has the power you give Him. No more. Nothing else.*

Those words spoken, the Old Man took a step forward, and was swallowed, immediately, by the darkness. He was gone, and it left the room in a deathly quiet. The noise, the howls, had stopped as soon as the Old Man stepped through that doorway. There was only the sound of footsteps, now: heavy boots on hard stone, receding, growing softer, quieter, almost gone, and then he heard the last one.

Time stopped, and ceased to have any meaning, as everything now seemed to happen all at once:

Thunder struck and echoed heavy, bouncing off and through the stone, emanating from everywhere all at once, the claps and booms joining together like waves crashing. The Kid was hit deep inside his chest by something like a profound loneliness made solid, and it threw him back, haphazardly, to the ground. The door was left to ruin—not collapsed or crumbled, it simply no longer existed in its previous state, and now fit more with the debris surrounding it, as though it had always existed as it was now.

The Kid's ears rang, his vision blurred, and the dust and smoke made it hard to get his bearings, which was becoming more important as the darkness came up from below, through what used to be a door, and spread toward him. Senses be damned, he scrambled to his feet, hoping to figure where there might be some safety. He saw—or maybe he'd noticed before and was just now bringing back to mind—a vestibule near the front of the antechamber, and he ran for it, fast as he could.

As soon as he was inside, he slid to the ground, braced himself—back against the far wall, feet against the door—hoping that would be enough to keep him safe, if such a concept were ever again to be an option. He covered his ears against the sounds, but not hearing, certainly, was not an option. The sounds welled up more from within than without, lived inside him, bounced back and forth in his head, giving him not a moment of relief as hard as he pressed his hands against its sides. Even with that cacophony inside himself, he could hear the deep, coughing sobs as he cried, unable to control himself, overwhelmed by the primordial feelings dredged up from hearing such a thing as a man should never hear. It overwhelmed and overstimulated, and there were no escape, and worse yet he caught a glint of light—of darkness—off a piece of shattered glass on the ground, out of the corner of his eye, and he was suddenly fixated.

There was no further concern about the sound of fire and ill; instead, it was that piece of a mirror, bright and clear, reflecting what little light there was, and the overwhelming desire to see it, to see what was in it. He forgot the sound and uncovered his ears—not that covering them had made any sort of difference—and reached for it. He wanted to see ... had to see. But before he could reach it, another explosion rattled the walls, sending the world again into turmoil. The Kid wanted out, but now, as though a mocking had been made of his environment, the vestibule door was stuck. He fought against it as much as he could muster before the howling started again, worse than before. Worse than the yell of any animal, worse than any noise that occurred in the natural world. His knuckles were white, like the bones themselves showed through under the skin, so tight did he hold that rifle. Tears streamed down from panicked eyes as he started—no, as he tried—to pray, but in those moments, with the sound and the fear and the knuckles, he couldn't remember any of the words.

There was another sound, now. It separated itself from the howls and shrieks, it cut through them all like thunder, though it was a muffled thing, rumbling up from under the ground instead of distant in the sky, and the Kid couldn't tell if this was thunder like he'd heard before from the pistols, or maybe something worse. It sent dust raining down upon him, making that small space feel even smaller, and then add to that the fact that the Kid knew he couldn't get out, and add again to that the walls began to rattle from some heavy impact, and it was that sense of powerlessness that left the Kid wondering what was gonna happen to him next, since it was clear now he wasn't in any kind of control over it, and that was the most terrifying feeling of all.

More thunder, and the Kid reacted like an animal, scrambling, throwing himself nails against stone, desperate to get out. No matter how hard he kicked, no matter how visceral his cries of pain and anguish and fear and fury, no matter how heavy the air which choked him was, no matter how hot he could feel the flames, crackling up through the darkness, no matter how chilling the howls became, growing closer, no matter how loud the screams that lived inside his own head, there was no escape. There was no use left in nothing, and the Kid couldn't take it.

The rifle's muzzle was under his chin before he'd had time to think about it too much. It snapped round in the same way it always did, the movements almost automatic, though he'd never made this particular movement before. He closed his eyes, not wanting to see the things around him and remember what was real, but instead preparing himself to embrace that long darkness; anything would be better than this. Eyes shut, he steeled himself, took a deep breath and held it … held it more, as the cacophony continued around him, every noise all at once.

Then, there was only one. Thunder, again—no, thankfully not from the rifle. A thunder that rang like an exclamation, silencing all other noises, letting the Kid hear clearly his own breath as he exhaled, and opened his eyes again to silence.

This specific silence seemed to last an eternity, which the Kid didn't mind so much, especially comparing it to the sounds what come before. Partially so's not to ruin the silence, and partially so's not to miss what was next, the Kid kept still. He waited, listening, almost like he didn't trust the silence, like he didn't believe it would last. And it didn't; for in that next moment, the vestibule door opened.

The Kid had to guard his eyes against the light what suddenly streamed in. He didn't bother to raise the rifle; he knew whatever opened that door, there weren't no use protecting himself. Whatever that figure was, silhouetted now in the doorway like that, the rifle wouldn't make a damn bit of difference.

*It's finished*, he finally heard the Old Man's voice say. That grip—
like cold iron—caught round his wrist and pulled the Kid to his
feet.

Once his eyes adjusted to the lack of darkness, the Kid realized
the entire church had been razed. No, not the entire church...
. That was a lie. The vestibule itself was still standing, totally
untouched, unbent and unbroken by whatever destruction had
accompanied the noise.

The same could not be said for the Old Man. He was battered,
beaten, clawed, and bitten. Blood—maybe his, maybe not—was
splayed and strewn about in no recognizable pattern. One of
those pistols were missing, the holster torn and ruined. Not
that it would have made much difference, since the Old Man's
opposite arm were in no state to still be called an arm, much
less hold a pistol. The remaining arm still held its weapon tight,
not because of any further need, but more that it was all the arm
could remember how to do, and were it to drop the damn thing
now there was a chance it weren't gonna be able to do much else
in the future.

The Kid was still shaking, still couldn't make out what had
happened, or even what might have happened. But there was
the one question that had been on his mind since he saw the Old
Man—one he figured he knew the answer to already, but had to
ask just in case.

*... He's gone?*

The Old Man was lost for a moment, somewhere else in his
thoughts, and he nodded.

*That's good, right?* the Kid followed, cautious with the question
like he almost didn't want the answer.

It took the Old Man a moment again to consider, and his arm awkwardly crossed his body to holster his remaining pistol as he answered. *There is no good. Not in matters like this.*

*But … it's over.* The Kid felt lost again, confused the same way he did when this whole thing started. Wasn't this the mission? Wasn't this the whole point of everything they'd done?

*Only just begun*, the Old Man replied, and he started walking—limping, hard—back down the spur. There weren't nothing resembling walls to differentiate inside from outside exactly, but after he'd crossed out of what used to be where the church stood, and before he fully disappeared from sight, the Kid saw the Old Man drop something. It was clear the Old Man likely hadn't done it on purpose, and certainly hadn't noticed it either way, so the Kid went to check on what it was.

A CROSS. THE KID PICKED UP the simple piece of silver by its leather thong; when it twirled around on its own he noticed the letter etched into its back. The Kid held it gently, traced his finger over the mottled "M," then tucked it away and followed the Old Man; there would be time to consider this more, to think on its meaning and ask as to its origins, later. For the moment, for the first time in their long journey together, he feared being left behind.

## 17. *The Plains Were Flat and Featureless*

WHAT HAPPENS NOW? THE KID asked, as they continued on the long way to nothing. It was the first words spoken by either man in some time, and the Kid had a feeling if he didn't speak first, nothing would be said for some time more.

*Lots to do, still. Best keep up.* The gruff, laconic nature of the Old Man's voice had been replaced with a forceful, hurried speech. Whereas before the Old Man always spoke like someone who was amused at having to answer the same question he'd been asked a dozen times before, this time he spoke with annoyance, like he expected the rest of the world to stay with him and didn't have time for explanations or niceties. It could be a subtle difference, but if, like the Kid had, you'd been so often on the receiving end of one, it became easy to tell when it turned in to the other.

Not long after, and through more silence—the Kid was right, as he didn't say anything and so nothing ended up being said— they reached a river. The Kid wasn't sure if it were the same river they'd seen before—maybe it was a tributary or branch or any of the other proper words for a different part of the same river— but whichever it was, at this point in its wide and wandering life, this river was miles across, barely moving, as though the current had given up pushing such a morass and just left the whole thing to its own devices, where if the water decided to move it would.

The Old Man limped along the bank, the Kid following as close as he thought was appropriate. The Old Man didn't move as fast as before, and the Kid was tired, so it all sort of evened out as these things go. What was strange—or, different, at least—is that not once did the Old Man ever look back, whether to check up, or make sure the Kid was okay, or any other reason. He had his place to go, and he didn't care who followed him. He certainly didn't seem to care when a pair of gunshots rang out from somewhere far away, across the other side of the river.

The Kid strained to see, but it was too gray, there was too much fog. *I thought He was gone?* the Kid said, and realized afterwards he hadn't necessarily meant to say out loud. It was a passing thought borne on the back of fear, and then the Kid started to worry maybe he was broken now, that every sound would create that sense of fear in him. But the Old Man didn't answer the question, and he didn't care about any of the Kid's concerns. He kept on.

Late into the evening, there was barely a sliver of moon, which was worse than nothing. What little light there was came through like tricks, using the clouds to create charades of every thing a man could be afeared of, and things he didn't know he should be. And it was just enough light to let you know a storm was coming. The Old Man limped along, steady, same as he had been. The Kid, exhausted, fought to keep up. He wanted to stop—he'd wanted to stop hours ago—but he knew if he did, the Old Man weren't gonna have no kinda sympathy and was gonna keep right on, and he would be left behind. And on a night like this, the Kid knew if he were to be left behind, there was never gonna be any catching up.

What stopped him was a creak, like an old door sliding open on its own accord, echoed low over the water. It was a lazy sound; nothing rushed, nothing pressing, but it still caused the Kid to snap round and look, and it was only then he could make out a massive shadow, looming in through the fog. The Old Man never looked, but simply stepped aside as if in a well-timed ballet as a ship—an old, wooden ship—ran aground, its bow cutting into and lifting up onto the sand.

The Kid weren't expecting it to arrive in any case, and he certainly wasn't expecting such a titanic and imposing structure to appear so close to him; it were far enough away he was safe, but close enough it was unnerving, and large enough he had to step back to get a full look at the thing, best he could through what was left of the fog, after the ship had pushed what it needed to aside. Its sails were torn to rags, hanging limp in the damp with no wind to cause them any movement. The entire hull were more pitch than wood at this point, and still there were gaping holes blown out of it, some just barely above the waterline. A man didn't have to know much about such things to know the ship had been abandoned for a long time; even the ratty and frayed rope ladder what hung over the side seemed to be trying to escape and get to shore, but the Old Man didn't see it like that. Without even testing the thing to see if it were safe, he grabbed hold and started to climb, almost in the same motion he'd stepped out of the way of the ship coming onto shore in the first place.

*Where are you going?* the Kid asked, as everything had happened so fast he didn't have time for any other questions.

*Where it takes me,* the Old Man responded, though just as he reached the edge of the deck, he thought a moment, then added, *Where I'm meant to be.*

After those words, the rain started. There was no pomp and circumstance, no clap of thunder, no nothing, just a heavy rain, coming down all at once, like a bucket poured into a trough … 'cept the bucket never emptied. So sudden, so overwhelming was it, that faster than should have been possible, the river began to rise, and with that started to pull the ship back off the shore. It all seemed like a set of well-choreographed maneuvers which the Kid weren't privy to, and he didn't let the surprise of it all blind him to the salient facts: the rope ladder would soon be out of reach, and the Kid would be left behind.

Like bringing his rifle around at the sight of dinner, he moved before he thought, ran and threw himself toward the ship, grabbed hold, and pulled himself up. It was a hard climb with a bad hand as he was suddenly reminded that he had, so he used what parts he could, the good bits of bone and sinew and the crooks of his joints, to fight his way up that frayed and unforgiving thing.

The state of the main deck wasn't a surprise, given what he'd seen from the ground. Every coiled rope would be useless in anything but a pile, all the wood was rotted, each cask broken, its contents a memory. Someone—or what used to be someone— was lashed to the wheel, long since dead, little more than bones remaining. It was there the Old Man stood, alongside this grim captain, and stared out at the river, as it was pounded by the sudden fury of the storm. The moon was hidden by the clouds, leaving little more than darkness and rain, but there was the Old Man, watching the world, watching something out there only he could see.

Or was it? The Kid joined him, looked out into the darkness, through the rain, to what little he could see of the river, and wondered if he could see it too. He looked, and watched, and saw past the darkness when a sliver of light turned to understanding, and the Kid realized …

*We're headed the wrong way.*

The Old Man never looked away from the river, and took a moment before he replied. *No. We ain't.*

But the Kid was certain. *Downriver should take us back to where your house was. Not far from it, leastways.*

*Things changed,* the Old Man said.

*What do you mean, "changed"?* the Kid prodded him, properly incredulous. This wasn't some cryptic lesson, this was plain wrong. *Rivers don't change,* he said, as though reminding the Old Man of a fact he shouldn't have forgotten.

*Everything changed.* It was, at least as the Old Man saw it, one of them cryptic lessons. And he felt like it was all what needed to be said.

But it wasn't. The Kid moved between the Old Man and the water—if he weren't fixin' to turn and look, if he were gonna keep staring down and out at that water, he was gonna have to see through the Kid to do it.

*We done what we came out here for, and now—*

The Old Man had him by the throat, quick as lightning.

*You done nothin'. You came to me and you asked for help, but you already knew the only part that mattered was yours. And I told you ye didn't have the mettle for it, and still you pushed on, and ye wouldn't hear the truth, and still ye dragged me down into the belly of the beast, and there you left it all for me.* The Old Man spit the words like fire, and once they was out, he threw the Kid, hard, leaving the Kid struggling to catch his breath from the grip and the impact both.

*And it ain't finished. There's still one part left to do.* The Old Man rubbed his forehead, his temples. The scars felt tight, and there weren't no relief. *Still one Seal left to open. Still quarrels to be settled, and war, and men with evil thoughts in their hearts.*

He let the words sit a moment, calmed himself, let the scars stop hurting, before he continued. *But I can put a stop to it. Bring some order to this world, finally. Undo all that's been done.* The Old Man's words made the Kid sick, and he stood up, angry, and took a step forward to recover his place.

*Now you're talking like Him.* And before the Kid could take that second step, there was a pistol to his forehead. No movement, nothing that could be called "fast," it was simply there. But the

Kid got his wish, and he was again staring into the eyes of the Old Man, and it was as though the darkness itself was reflected in them.

*Well, He was right.*

The Kid didn't look away, and the two men spent a lifetime in that moment, in that gaze. Neither bent nor broke, but it was the Kid who spoke first.

*I ain't gonna let you do this.*

A soft click, and the Old Man lowered the hammer with his thumb, then holstered the gun.

*You ain't gonna stop me. Not now. You already had your test, and ye failed.* Casually, the Old Man pushed the Kid aside, and let his blank stare again lay out upon the water.

*Good thing ye failed.*


## 18. Belowdecks

THE KID SAT IN A small storeroom, sitting on the only crate that was still sturdy enough to be called such. In turn, the rifle sat across'd his lap, and he fed its cartridges into it one after another, lost in thoughts as he was. The cross he'd found now hung loosely from his neck, and bobbed with each slight movement he made. It turned sharply, ever so slightly revealing that "M" etched into the back, when the Kid turned quick as he heard a clatter outside the room. It was close enough he couldn't ignore it, and he was up and off that crate, out through the narrow doorway, and into the dark hold beyond.

The leaks were worse here, and the wood under the Kid's feet was soft and rotten, where each step threatened to send him through the floor into whatever lay below. The only parts which weren't wet were sticky with pitch, spilled haphazard-like, as though that would do any good 'cept make it harder to walk, as though a man should be walking here. The Kid reached his hand up around in the rafters, feeling for something he thought he'd seen out the corner of his eye when he came down this way in the first place, and sure enough, there it was, wedged in tight slightly askew from how he'd remembered: a lantern. He felt through his pockets, and quicker than he would have guessed found that ol' lighter he'd managed to keep with him this whole time, and a bit awkward, seeing as how both his hands were mostly otherwise occupied, he shook it to make sure.... .

Empty? That weren't right. He shook it again, as though that would change the outcome, and tried the damn thing anyway, just in case. Nothing came the first time, and similarly the second, and the Kid knew there weren't no use in trying a third, and no time to contemplate doing anything else, since a creak of the wood sounded nearby—different from the creak and bow that he'd heard before, this was something more, something different. Something moving in its own way, rather than the way everything else was.

Far from panicking, the Kid closed his eyes, calm, hopeful, and whispered something even he couldn't hear, words he wasn't sure he'd known before. He tried it one more time, and turns out there was use in that, as the wick sparked and flamed to life, if just barely. He couldn't hide the smile before he opened his eyes, that little triumph of fire dancing in front of his face, and quickly put that to the lantern, lest it decided its job were done. Granted, what dim light the lantern decided it would give didn't help much, but it were better, and it gave the Kid a chance to search around what he could.

As far as the small radius of what could barely be called light would reveal to him, there weren't much more down here than the same barrels of rotten grain and coils of ratty, overworn rope that he'd seen earlier. There were small patches of pitch trying desperately to hold back the damp of the wood that maybe he hadn't paid all that much attention to, but the general idea of what all was around him weren't much different. And just before he began to wonder if he'd needed this lantern at all, and if he'd wasted that last little spark he might ever have asked for from the lighter,  he saw a glint of something across the hold. It wasn't something easy to make out at this distance, but only a handful of things would give off a glint against the light, all of them a thing he would be interested in, and so the Kid moved toward it, slowly, each step creaking, though a different kind of noise, a different speed and intent than the one he'd heard earlier, and both of them different from the ebb and flow of creaks the ship itself resounded here in its belly. And when the Kid made his way far enough that his little radius of light suddenly became useful, he saw it: a table, set for a meal, though clearly never used, and every piece of the place setting somehow intact, unmoved, unshaken by the creaking and movement and swaying and damp. The glint had come from a spoon—polished silver, untarnished—and the Kid picked it up, examined it. As he turned it just the right way, it caught the light, and it caught his reflection, and the Kid seen himself for the first time in what felt like ages, and what by now had been.

IT WAS STILL HIM. HIS face. Everything he recognized. But there was something else there with him.

Darkness, looming in the spaces behind. Not the simple absence of light, but darkness in a form all its own. A quick glance over the shoulder revealed … darkness, certainly, but the plain old darkness leaves when the lights go out. No, what he saw in the reflection, that was different.

The Kid had to know for sure. He turned the silver once again to catch the light, to see that reflection …

And there it was. Right on top of him now. Taking shape. Twisting itself. Hardening.

Waiting for him.

The Kid's hand trembled so, and he couldn't help but drop the spoon; where it landed back onto the table, in its rightful place, it made a hell of a clatter—the same sound what drew him out in the first place. And with that clatter the lantern was snuffed, and suddenly that plain old darkness was everywhere again, too. Fear came with it, as the two usually travel hand in hand, but the Kid smiled, instead, and held it back. Maybe he couldn't control the darkness without help—without the lantern—but the fear was his alone.

With that at bay, he could focus, could hear the footsteps coming closer, the creaking—that other kind of creaking, what he'd heard before—rolling low across the air and coming closer.

*Always knew there was something out there, waitin' for me to become it.* The Old Man's voice was of the darkness, coming from all around, all at once. The Kid had heard sounds like this before.

*You had it wrong, you know,* the Kid replied, confidently now, because he knew the Truth. He had that lighter at hand again, and readied to strike it. He didn't have to close his eyes or say the words. He knew what would happen, when it was time.

*But I was afraid. I hid from it. I didn't want to have to face Him again. Not alone.* The Old Man's voice wasn't closer, exactly, since it was already everywhere at once, but the creaking had stopped.

*You have to embrace it,* the Kid said, and he scratched the lighter so's that tiny flame came back to life. He tossed it aside, let it skitter across the floor, right to where he knew the pitch and that wet rot had met in a once-epic confrontation, lost forever now that the pitch caught fire, and those flames roared to life instead'a being held back in that tiny wick as they'd been, as it spread wide, in a flash.

*I was selfish. I prayed for another, so I wouldn't have to shoulder the burden Myself.* The Old Man was almost apologetic in His words. Wherever He was, He hadn't moved since the flames started.

*You have to be strong enough to take it inside you. To keep it safe.* The Kid took a step away from the table, toward where he thought the Old Man might have been, but an unseen blow threw him to the ground. There, the fire crept up to surround him, but the Kid remained unhurt—for the moment—and welcomed the warmth.

*That ain't fair,* the Old Man continued, His words catching in his throat, now. *I can't ask you to become that.*

*It's a part of us,* the Kid replied, reassuring, and stood back to his feet. Though he couldn't see, the darkness now punctuated by the smoke, all surrounding him, holding him close, the Kid brought that rifle to his shoulder.

*It ain't your burden.* The Old Man's voice cracked again, and the Kid wondered if he could see Him, if He wouldn't maybe be crying.

*But we must embrace it,* the Kid said, and pushed the stock tight to his cheek as he looked down the iron sights. *We must become the darkness.*

The Kid saw it, now, at the end of the barrel. It weren't no longer the Old Man, but something else. Darkness. Fear. Hatred. All taken form, and growing. Getting closer. His outstretched hands were the fire and the smoke, all getting closer, what then wrapped around the Kid's neck, just like he'd seen—dreamt?— so long before. But this time, there weren't no fear. There weren't no choking or gasping for breath, or wont to change the thing; the rifle clattered to the floor. The Kid stood serene and welcomed it, embraced what had been the Old Man, and pulled Him closer. Held Him.

The Old Man, that darkness, panicked now. Tried to let go, tried to push away, but this time, it was His actions that weren't no use. The Kid pulled closer, wrapped his arms around what should have been His form; loving, understanding. Once they was close enough, the Kid whispered in His ear. Words of forgiveness, as the flames swallowed them.

The river stopped. The ship, now still, was engulfed by flames. Embers lit the air as the wood burned away to nothing, leaving only black smoke where there had once been so much.

**And for some time thereafter, it was quiet.**

## 19. *The Slow Current of the River*

IT WAS A NEW DAY. The drifting water was clear, the sun high and bright. On the riverbank, atop a bed of fine, soft sand, the Kid woke with a start, a racking cough clearing his lungs of what water was left in them.

It took him a moment to realize how utterly confused he was about the unfamiliar surroundings, to acknowledge he had no idea how he'd gotten here, or where here was, exactly. So he did what any reasonable person would do: he stood up out of that sand and wiped himself clean best he could, then checked his pockets, wondering if he had anything on him that might be useful. The only thing he found was that cross, still around his neck, still bobbing gently, reminding him of its presence with each movement, subtle or grand.

There, too, nearby on the ground, was that rifle of his, which he picked up and cleaned off best he could, even though whatever damage the fine sand was liable to do had already been done, which he would just have to sort out later. He had no pack, nowhere to put it, so over his shoulder it was.

The Kid started walking along to follow the current, as long as that way might be.

By the time he reached it, the farmhouse was much the same as before. In the doorway, the Kid stared at the chest, at its ancient locks, and his head hung heavy with his thoughts. Heavier still as he knelt, and in a solemn moment removed that cross, pressed it to his lips, and whispered the only words he could think were appropriate.

*I'm sorry.*

The Kid placed the cross inside, where it belonged, and the rifle went next, though it barely fit. He then dragged that heavy old thing back out to the storm cellar, though he decided to give himself a break from the stairs right this moment, and promised he'd come back to store it away proper sometime later, before it got dark.

For the moment, then, he went out to the trough, which he found empty and dry. Odd enough, the corn had come up strong and ripe, not only out in the fields but in the pen, next to the trough, around the house. The rain had helped, and when the Kid went to check one of the ears closest to him, he found it plump and healthy. He was about to pick one when he heard a snort, in amongst a thickness of stalks just on the side of the fence there. When he hurried to push past them, he saw that one pig—he never would have known it was sick, once, but the Old Man would have remembered her—healthy now. She'd survived, and she'd spent all this time eating her fill, as had her seven little ones, which busied themselves rooting and playing … or, what passes for playing, with pigs. Their play seemed mostly to consist of rushing into stalks, then attacking any fallen corn, nipping and butting at one another for the choicest kernels. All in good fun, as it was with pigs, as there was plenty to go around.

A hammer and rusty nails did their best against the fence, and the pigs, fat and content enough to cooperate, for now, were back in their pen; their trough full, the ground moist and cool, there was nowhere else they'd rather be. The Kid kept his promise, and by the time dusk came, the chest were back in its rightful place, and the storm cellar door had gotten the hammer and rusty nail treatment, and the Kid took a moment to sweep the last of the dust out, from off the porch.

A few well-placed lanterns lit the place, and the Kid washed up in a bucket of fresh, clean water, before checking himself in that mirror, its paper and fabric taken down and stored for another task, another time. He used the same spoon to finish the same bowl of mostly cooled mash before he knelt at the side of that same simple bed, whispering to himself words he barely remembered, but knew they were the Truth.

And from outside, with darkness all around, light came in a tiny flicker, through a small window.

# ABOUT THE AUTHOR

**DALAN MUSSON** IS A FORMER independent-circuit professional wrestler whose screenwriting credits include Marvel Studios' *The Falcon and The Winter Soldier*. This is his first novel.

CPSIA information can be obtained
at www.ICGtesting.com
Printed in the USA
BVHW042330300623
666612BV00008B/483